PRAISE FOR *A QUIT

An *Electric Literature* Bes
An NPR Critics Summer Pick · A *Good Morning*
America Pick of the Month · A Michelle Obama's
Reach Higher Summer Reading List Pick ·
A Goodreads Big Buzz Debut · A Tertulia
Staff Pick of the Month

"Compelling . . . Chang's storytelling is beautifully subtle, often studded with sublime wit." —KIA CORTHRON,
New York Times Book Review

"A deep, propulsive, poignant, and unflinching portrayal of a family in all of its mystery." —SAM LIPSYTE,
author of *No One Left to Come Looking for You*

"A drolly comedic tale . . . reminiscent of Rachel Khong's *Goodbye, Vitamin* and Weike Wang's *Chemistry*." —LELAND CHEUK,
NPR

"A riveting, wise, and singular novel about grief, love, longing, and the mysteries of family, *A Quitter's Paradise* will linger in your heart and mind." —JESSAMINE CHAN,
author of *The School for Good Mothers*

"Calls to mind recent explorations of science and relationships, including Weike Wang's *Chemistry* and Brandon Taylor's *Real Life*." —KEZIAH WEIR,
Vanity Fair

"A sharp, intimate, and poignant investigation of grief, family dynamics, and selfhood." —*Electric Literature*

A QUITTER'S PARADISE

A Novel

ELYSHA CHANG

SJP LIT
A zando IMPRINT

NEW YORK

The characters and events in this book are fictitious. Any similarity to real persons, living or dead, is coincidental and not intended by the author.

SJP Lit is an imprint of Zando
zandoprojects.com

Originally published in hardcover by SJP Lit, June 2023
First trade paperback edition, April 2024

Text design by Aubrey Khan, Neuwirth & Associates, Inc.
Cover design by Evan Gaffney

The publisher does not have control over and is not responsible
for author or other third-party websites (or their content).

Library of Congress Control Number: 2022946766

978-1-63893-161-4 (Paperback)
978-1-63893-053-2 (ebook)

10 9 8 7 6 5 4 3 2 1
Manufactured in the United States of America

for my parents

Explorer, you tell yourself this is not what you came for

Although it is good here, and green;

You had meant to move with a kind of largeness,

You had planned a heavy grace, an anguished dream.

—GWENDOLYN MacEWEN

A
QUITTER'S
PARADISE

1

Late one morning a young man and his wife find an egg in front of their garage. The next morning, they find another. The eggs are small and blue, and their shells are cracked open. Their milky contents have hardened on the asphalt.

What is this? Some kind of curse? the wife asks.

Teens, maybe, the husband says. He searches the face of the house for other signs of idle vandalism but doesn't find anything.

That night, it's warm out. The couple sleeps close, with the windows open. They're woken up at dawn by a birdcall. Breathless and incessant, a high-whistle alarm.

The hell, the husband mutters into his pillow.

Outside, a robin is zigging and zagging at the garage, worrying the edges, looking for a way in. The wife runs down, hefts the garage door open, and the frantic bird flies to an overhead shelf in the far corner. Turns out there is a nest there, two blue eggs already in progress.

Can you imagine? Wife's eyes are wet and round when she returns upstairs. Needing to lay an egg but having to keep it in because you can't get home? And then it just falls out of you and smashes on the ground?

The husband lets out a laugh, invites his wife back to bed with an outstretched arm. Yeah. Terrible. Holding in a shit like that.

．　．　．

This is a story I used to tell at parties and social gatherings, back when we went to them. Our friends in the city loved hearing about animal intruders, the little dramas of our life in the suburbs. Ellis always rolled his eyes when I got to his line. "I never said anything like that."

I winked at whoever was listening. "My memory's not the best," I told them.

Possibly it does feel like holding in a shit. I wouldn't know. I have never been pregnant, and I've never studied a bird. In college, I worked as a lab assistant, training marmosets to focus their eyes on certain shapes on a screen. Later, in graduate school at Mount Sinai, I spent two years observing aggressive behavior in female fruit flies.

The Mount Sinai neuroscience program was where I met Ellis, a fourth-year PhD who had already coauthored two papers on optogenetics and pain resistance in mice. Others in the program wryly called him a "rising star." We weren't a particularly competitive group, but we were all very wry.

I met Ellis at a New Year's Eve party in one of the massive duplex dorm apartments on 97th and Park. He was tall and thin, shaped like a dying tree. In the early hours of the night, we had a long conversation about our siblings and birth order, nature and nurture, books we had seen on the hostess's shelves, which I didn't think was all so painful, but which he ended abruptly, "Hey. Are you just the quiet type or should I leave you alone? I'm fine either way. I just like things to be clear."

Afterward, we emailed. Ellis and I worked on the same campus. We didn't have to email. We could easily have gotten coffee or drinks or sat stupidly with frozen yogurt. But I am circumspect when it comes to love, and I appreciated that Ellis seemed to sense this about me.

He sent long, well-crafted messages asking about my research goals, offering words of advice, inquiring about my musical tastes and, as our conversations progressed, my previous relationships.

I hadn't dated, really, since high school and had gradually stopped listening to music after college. But this hardly seemed appealing, so I made false reference to a recent amicable breakup and said I was generally open to any musical genre except Broadway.

We took to exchanging images of our work. I sent him confocal representations of the motor neurons in fruit fly vaginas. He sent me comparison charts of rat brain slices ordered by size and section. They looked like phases of the moon.

We sent each other photos of our families on budget beach vacations, of our teen selves posing awkwardly with wind instruments and sports equipment. After about two weeks, I sent a photo of my bare ass, taken in front of the bathroom mirror and cropped to a small, disembodied close-up. It didn't look like much. Rounded flesh in front of blue and white tiles. But he wrote back right away: What about the front?

2

I recall my mother groaning when I told her about Ellis and the picture of my butt. We were sitting at the butcher block table in her kitchen, peeling garlic and dropping the bare cloves in a plastic tub. This was two years ago, when she was still alive and still had the energy to cook for herself.

"Why torture me?" she said. "Is this what modern girls do now?" She grabbed another bulb from the bowl. The papery skins rustled against each other and made a pleasant scratching sound. Strands of dim orange hair fell in front of her face.

I shrugged, laughing. "I thought it was funny."

"Your jokes. Do people laugh at them?" she asked in earnest.

No, I admitted, they did not.

We kept on peeling. My mother asked if I would stay for dinner, though she knew I always did. Every Sunday, I arrived for lunch, we did some afternoon activity, and then had dinner before I took the train back into the city. The activity ranged from watching old movies and falling asleep beside each other on the couch to sharpening all the knives with an industrial sharpener I borrowed from a friend.

On the days I visited, my mother's caretaker, Jiajia, was always away for the day. Off at her other job where she assisted an acupuncturist who lived and worked from his home office nearby. Jiajia had orbited my family since we were children. She had worked for my father and lived in his warehouse, then lived with my mother for years after Jiajia's father died. I was grateful to her for caring for my mother, but for the most part we avoided each other.

That afternoon, the air inside was thick, as if a window needed to be opened. But outside, it was wet, too, so I didn't bother. It was a warm, muggy spring. The sycamore leaves were just beginning to bud on the very ends of tree branches, like small green afterthoughts.

"Do I get to see a picture of this man? This emailer?"

I didn't want to show her. My mother had a habit of ruining the things that I loved. Or, worse, the things I was just beginning to love. And I was never able to resist her. I felt that she made me smarter and better for all the ways she could critique a person. Skewer and lay bare their flaws. It was her way of loving me.

"Here." I handed her my phone. Having done my research, I was acutely aware of every photo of Ellis that was publicly available online. This one was the least informative. Ellis stood squarely in front of a brick wall, squinting at the light behind the photographer. Below his photo were his lab role and italicized credentials. He had long, doll-like eyelashes. Freckles the color of his lips dotted his cheeks and forehead. His mouth was spread into a thin smile, but his brow was stern and lowered in the sun. It gave his face an unnerving, paradoxical look.

My mother stared at the photo. She had that dreadful look on her face, like she was divining something.

"He's handsome," I offered. Now it was her turn to offer something.

"Same job as you? Same career?"

I explained that he was a few years ahead in the program.

A low grumble rose from her throat. "What is he? Italian?"

"He's Greek."

She nodded. "Almost Italian."

"Am I almost Korean?"

"To the Italians, yes. And what's this?" She pointed at a mole between Ellis's eyebrows.

"I don't know, Ma. What do you think?"

She zoomed in on the photo with great and unnecessary precision. Like she had found something precious. Something sparkling, buried deep in soil.

"A mark in the middle of the face." She shook her head. "Inauspicious."

I tried simply to forge ahead. "He's very smart, not that you asked. One of the most accomplished people in the program."

Mom narrowed her eyes at the photo, as if my defense made him all the more suspect.

"I always thought *you* were the most accomplished person in the program."

"I don't know where you got that idea."

"He should get this removed." She pointed at the spot on his face.

"Ugh, Ma."

"What ugh? Why ugh? You want my honest opinion? He's not marriage material."

"Marriage? Who said anything about getting married? How did we get here?" My fingertips were wet, and I took the phone back from her between both wrists. "I'm just telling you about my life. A random person in my life."

She gave me a thin, caustic laugh. "Daughter, I'm dying." She grabbed the last bone-white clove and cracked it apart. "Why use up my time with nonsense?"

3

Ellis and I were married that same year at the city clerk's office on a wet Thursday in October. Brown and orange leaves tumbled at every disordered direction of the wind, leaving dark marks on the legs of Ellis's pants and the hem of my coat. It was my twenty-fourth birthday.

It felt thrilling and illicit being there without our families. Sometimes it's easy to do something cowardly and confuse it for being bold. Anyway, it was what Ellis and I had agreed upon. A ceremony for just the two of us. Something that would be remembered by us, privately, and no one else.

The clerk who married us was a round-faced woman with a large flat smile. Her canines had been shaved in such a way that her teeth formed a perfectly straight line.

When it was our turn, she asked if I was nervous.

I told her I wasn't.

She nodded knowingly. There was a glossy Bakelite sloth pinned to the lapel of her jacket. "Today is your day," she said. "Enjoy it."

I was bothered by her familiarity and would have preferred to keep things professional. But I was wearing the ridiculous ivory pantsuit I had borrowed from my roommate and there was a nest of white taffeta pinned unsteadily to my head. I was not in a position to do anything but smile.

"There she is," the clerk said.

Ellis squeezed my hand.

Afterward, we celebrated with dim sum on Mott Street. Ellis was jolly and overpolite with every cart-hauler who stopped by our table. "We just got married," he explained to the young server refilling our tea. He nodded and paid us an indifferent smile.

"Did you need anything else?" the server said.

"It's also her birthday, man," Ellis said, flush-faced from the celebratory whiskey we had been discreetly pouring into our teacups.

The man wished me a happy birthday, and I thanked him. Then, he brought us the check.

4

That week, I packed up my belongings and moved into Ellis's house, a squat Victorian in Matawan he was in the long process of refurbishing.

Generally, I was happy. A short courting period is risky but not unheard of. And on the rare occasion that I worried we had moved too quickly, Ellis would soothe me with clichéd sayings of such earnest assurance that I couldn't summon the critical faculties to say anything against them.

"We just love each other," he might say, tugging at the lobe of my ear. Or, "Some things are simple if you just allow them to be," nudging a knee between my legs.

Yes. I would allow them to be, I told myself. I felt myself opening toward a new way of being. Ellis's way. Things could be simple, happy, if only I let them.

The main obstacle to my simple, happy life, according to Ellis, was that I was prone to secret-keeping. Specifically, that I had not yet told my mother we were married.

Weeks passed. Every Sunday, I went dutifully to her house. (A much easier trip now that I myself lived in New Jersey.) Together, we wrapped dumplings, we salted the driveway for snow. We dropped her car at the dealership, we visited a jewelry show at the convention center. She was already sick, but not so sick that we couldn't pretend she was well. She hadn't moved downstairs to the first-floor bedroom yet, for instance. And Jiajia still cooked only some meals and kept the house clean.

There just never was the right opportunity. I didn't talk about Ellis, which was the surest sign that I was still seeing him. She didn't ask about him, which was the surest sign that she knew. It wasn't just Ellis. I habitually did not talk to my mother about men I was beginning to love. She had a habit of ruining my relationships from one side—pecking at them with her cynic's view of marriage until I eventually/inevitably saw things her way.

"But you're already married to me. So, what are you afraid she'll do, exactly?" Ellis asked.

I had just returned home from a fifth Sunday with my mother without telling her the news.

"What mother wouldn't be excited about her adult daughter getting married? You're happy, you're taken care of, loved." I could hear the flint of resentment in his voice.

I tried to imagine my mother squealing with animal pleasure at the news of my marriage, the way Ellis's mom had when we'd visited his parents the day before. I envisioned her stamping her slippered feet, taking my hands in her smaller ones and leading me to the leather couch where she would ask to hear all about the ceremony, about the man I had yoked myself to, about our plans for the future. Oddly, I was actually able to eke out the image. In my lifetime, I have watched too much network TV.

. . .

In the end, I bit the bullet and texted her a picture of our marriage license, a flimsy document with a faintly embossed seal. With my thumbnail, I covered the date. It had been six weeks. No use adding insult to injury.

My mother called within a few minutes. "What is this? One of your jokes?"

"Surprise," I said.

For a while, there was silence between us. I could hear that she wasn't at home. In the distance, there was the sound of metal clattering. She was at an auto shop, or near some grocery carts.

"Are you by yourself? Is Jiajia with you?"

"Who am I to you? A stranger?"

"Ma, you shouldn't be out alone."

"You're the one always leaving me alone. Who am I? A nobody? An enemy? These are the people you keep out of your life. I'm dead to you already. Is that it?"

"Stop. It's just something Ellis and I decided on together. It was important for us to do it alone. His parents weren't there either."

Her voice was muffled; she was speaking to someone else.

"Hello? Ma."

"How did I raise you to be so foolish? What's the rush to marry? You'll regret this, my daughter. That's all I can say."

I felt pretty numb to this; she was always hexing what I did by mapping her regrets onto mine. She'd regretted being married, but why did that mean that I would?

"Everything he is, you will not be. That is what happens when two become one. He's the successful one, you said? What will that make you?"

"I'll be okay," I offered. I wanted to reassure her. Wouldn't anyone? "We'll take care of each other. We love each other."

"Your Chinese," she said. "It's terrible. Gotten worse."

5

I discovered in marriage that Ellis had wild amounts of energy. Our first year together, he first- and coauthored paper after paper, worked nights, weekends. Every evening, he came home smiling and, for some reason, sweating from all his achievements at the lab.

He graduated the year after we were married and, to our delight, secured a postdoc at the lab where I worked. At the time, optogenetics was very new. His research had received a good deal of press and become a steady recipient of federal and international grants and graduate assistant applications. Friends and old colleagues joked that he had surpassed the level of rising star: he was a comet now.

Meanwhile, my research stalled. I was beginning to find it wasteful and tiresome, this endless slicing and staining and studying of mouse cortexes—all to prove a conjecture I myself had made up, seemingly out of thin air. Either that or I found myself hewing too closely to what already existed. What had already been proven, or what others were asking to have re-proven and corroborated.

I couldn't find the perfect balance, as every other third-year seemed to be doing. I'd accumulated hours of data, observation, imaging, recording. But was I any closer to identifying a pattern? A meaningful narrative about an inbred mouse's brain (much less a human one)? I submit that I was not. My research was in constant need of direction and guidance from my PI, and still I was unable to make any particular headway.

What was its purpose? This nagging question had surfaced as an afterthought, but now it was unraveling the rest of my career. Plus, it had started tugging away at other areas of my life. It became difficult to summon the energy to shower each morning, to ask Ellis each afternoon what he thought he might want to eat for dinner, to spend days and nights in the lab. Purpose, which I so wished to find, eluded me.

I left the program after my third year with a master's degree in hand, essentially announcing that I had failed to complete the doctoral program. Briefly, I entertained a job with a neurotech venture capitalist firm in Delaware. I wrote a handful of articles for an online outlet about consciousness, started working on a pop science book, and, ultimately, asked Ellis to hire me as a lab tech. Every comet has its tail.

. . .

The good thing about working as my husband's lab tech is that I can still pursue my research but without the pressure of expiring grants or an overly demanding PI or having to come to some replicable, meaningful conclusion about the brain and how it works. I can pursue it as long as it interests me and as long as I pay for any of the atypical materials myself.

Ellis and I have an agreement. I perform the duties of a lab technician (animal husbandry, analysis, some of the paper drafting and data visualization), and in return I'm free to study what I like and use his grant money for reasonable tools and equipment.

Penny, my former PI, frowns on this arrangement. She pulled me aside last year and asked if this was really what I wanted. "What if you find something? Who gets the credit? Ellis?" Her face twisted up like a wrung towel. "You're not a tech, Eleanor," she said. "You're a scientist. A good one. Who gave up."

This spoke to my ego, though it shouldn't have. Some days it was enough to have my intelligence recognized without having to pursue it to its ends. Wasn't this, my ego leapt to justify, the absence of ego?

"It's also a matter of accountability," Penny went on. "Attaching your name to something. It's a matter of taking responsibility. You won't get anywhere just dabbling around like this." To Ellis, she called it a misuse of valuable lab resources. But we didn't care. Ellis's postdoc was funded entirely by the NIH, which meant he, and not Penny, had full control over how it was apportioned.

Yes, I have had to face the fact that I quit. I have had to watch as my friends, now in their fourth year, settle into their labs and their research projects. But I'm not ashamed. Generally, I'm content. There's hope for quitters, too. There's a paradise on the other side of giving up.

The Great Machine

When Eleanor Liu was seven years old, she found a white cat lazing in the sun on the splintered front porch of her house. This thing was small, with a thick feral tail. She had seen it once before around the neighborhood, or maybe in a cartoon on TV. It wore a blue collar, from which dangled a brassy, tinkling bell.

Eleanor had always wanted a pet, but her parents staunchly refused to get one. They both agreed that animals had no place in the home unless that home was a farm, and the animals were its laborers. Plus, what did Eleanor know about animals? Nothing. She and her older sister often watched programs featuring drooling dogs and scheming cats, but beyond this, her experience was limited.

Narisa was two years older than Eleanor, and far more adventurous and reckless, which meant that Eleanor spent a great deal of her childhood doing adventurous and reckless things she did not enjoy (passing a basketball back and forth while rollerblading down the narrow street, squatting over potted plants and pissing in them "like boys do" (though Eleanor had never seen a boy do this)).

Eleanor stepped toward the cat, and it moved away—not fearful, just disinterested. She reached out her hand and sang a little song, a short one about body parts that she had learned in school. The cat's ears flickered, and Eleanor kept singing the body song, repeated it over and over again and didn't stop, even when the cat came to her, brushed soft and warm against her leg, its bell chiming softly. Eleanor could hardly contain herself. She had called the cat with a song, and the cat had come!

Inside, Eleanor's mother peeled vegetables for a broth, which they would eat for dinner that night. From the window by the kitchen sink, she watched as her daughter sang to some other family's cat.

Rita shook her head and sighed, loudly as if someone (anyone) was in the kitchen with her. Her daughter was too mild, she diagnosed as she dropped the long daikon scraps in the trash. Over time, this mildness would become weakness and gullibility, she nodded thoughtfully as she sliced the peeled root into thin white pucks. And these qualities in turn would make Eleanor a very unhappy woman.

A stumped end of the daikon, rotted at its edges, sailed through the air. It smacked the head of the intruding cat, and, for a moment, Rita was impressed with her own accuracy. The cat made its animal yelp and ran home to its family, a more leisurely one that did not mind an additional, though useless, mouth to feed.

"Stew for dinner," Rita called from the window. "Come help." She pushed the contents of her cutting board into a pot. Eleanor said nothing, watched the cat saunter off. She was young, only seven, and her childish faith in others was not so unusual then. All things had their logic, she supposed, even those she couldn't understand.

. . .

The Liu family lived in Sayreville, New Jersey, about a ten-mile drive from New Brunswick. They occupied a blue clapboard house that faced west, away from the man-made canal that carried water from the cooling station of a nuclear plant in Louisa Township to a warm-water reservoir nearby called Lake Anna. Down the street from the Liu house was the abandoned East Sayreville trailer park, which was believed among the town's children to be haunted by the ghosts of the murdered Riccio family but known among Sayreville's older teens as a place to buy drugs that came in from the city.

This abandoned lot was where a teenaged Narisa spent much of her spare time, which she had a great deal of. Unlike

Eleanor, Narisa's afternoons were not filled with productive activities like basketball practice (to make Eleanor stronger) and acting classes (to make Eleanor louder). Narisa was already too strong, as far as her mother was concerned. She behaved badly and made bad grades and was often scolded in school and at home for being brash and disruptive.

As a child, Narisa harbored a tendency toward violence. She would shove Eleanor against the chain-link fence that bordered the canal, which ran along a leg of their walk home from school. Or she might just kick at the backs of Eleanor's heels if she felt her sister was walking too slowly. On one occasion at the kitchen table, Narisa gripped Eleanor's arm suddenly, rubbed the dull serrations of a butter knife against her skin. Why?

Eleanor squirmed.

"Move! Try harder," Narisa commanded as she held Eleanor's wrist against the table. "You're just going to sit there?"

When Eleanor finally got away, she held her wrist to her chest. She checked for blood but was embarrassed to find the knife had only broken through a few layers of skin.

"That's all?" Narisa scoffed as tears formed in Eleanor's eyes. "You know, if we were animals, you'd be dead already."

Was this rivalry? Was Narisa jealous of the attention and resources that their mother paid to Eleanor? Not really. It seemed natural to Narisa that the family was split in two halves—their mother loving Eleanor as if she were a doll that had arrived at the house in parts, and their father loving

Narisa by bringing her gifts from his trips to Taiwan (silken scarves, fine hairpins made of ox bone, snow globes from various airports).

There were gifts for Eleanor, too, but it escaped neither sister that Narisa's were always larger and more beautiful. Mr. Liu claimed that the reason was because Narisa was older, but Eleanor and Narisa both sensed that he simply loved Narisa more. Rita understood this, too. Jing, she felt, was part of the problem.

Liu Jing was an importer of wigs and hair accessories and the owner of a modest warehouse at the intersection of Casequake Avenue and Della Street. The enterprise was small but sufficient. On staff were a few workers whose numbers fluctuated depending on the season. They combed and packaged wigs, beaded and tied ribbons which they glued to thin metal clips. These products were then packed and distributed (usually by Jing himself) to buyers in the Garment District.

Summers, Jing traveled to Taipei where he sought new suppliers and renewed or shed existing contracts. His trusted man on the ground was Ah Mao, his younger brother. Often these summer trips extended well into September, and he returned to New Jersey just in time for Eleanor's birthday and the rush of last-minute Christmas orders.

After his few months away, Jing would return as unceremoniously as he had departed. The girls would come home from school to find him seated on the cracked leather couch reading the *World Journal*. Or unclogging some drain or gutter that they hadn't thought to look at while he was gone.

Rita complained to Jing that these routine absences troubled their children, but the truth was they troubled her more than they did her daughters. This cycle of intermittent absence was something Narisa and Eleanor accepted with docility and understanding. These were the comings and goings that gave the Liu family its rhythm. There were the times with Dad, and there were the times with No Dad.

If they had been asked to choose, both girls would have said that their mother was the more troubling parent of the two. When Jing was at home, Rita minded them the old-fashioned way. She cooked, she cleaned. She nipped at them for being too thin and, later, too fat. She hovered as they did their homework at the butcher block kitchen table, comparing their assignments and work ethic unfavorably to those of her own school days.

But when Jing left, she morphed into someone else completely. She could spend hours in her bedroom, watching TV, listening to Chyi Yu or other such songstresses on cassette. The air in her room soured with the smell of cigarette smoke. Some days she wandered along the canal or into town, took photographs with a black camera that hung heavy around her neck. She bought a bicycle. She rode it only when he wasn't around. The camera swung forth and back, hitting her in the chest.

It couldn't be described as a façade that Rita maintained, or a pose she reserved exclusively for Jing. It was something more alchemical than that. Jing brought some other part of her to life. His presence had the ability to animate her, though his absence did, too.

One afternoon, the girls came home from school to find that she had dyed her hair orange. It was cruel to laugh at her, but they were young and did it anyway.

"It looks . . ." Eleanor started.

"Like your head is on fire," Narisa answered.

"Okay." Rita shrugged. She balled up a coupon for a large pan pizza and threw it in their general direction. It lay like a crumpled flower on the bright white kitchen tile. "You think I care? I don't rely on either of you to be happy," she said. "I rely on myself. I'm free."

Briefly, Rita waited for them to say something, and when neither of them did, she opened the freezer. A plume of cold air came out as she sighed, unearthed a heavy plastic bag of frozen dumplings. She threw them one at a time into a pot of water. Later, Eleanor would forget about this exchange. Narisa would wonder if her mother was having an affair.

When Jing returned in the fall, so did Rita. She cooked square meals again and prescribed her daughters with remedies for various non-ailments. Butterfish broth for Narisa's flat chest. Coconut oil rubs for Eleanor's eczema. She cleaned the house and made the beds. She stocked the girls' bathroom with soap and shampoo.

Needless to say, Narisa and Eleanor grew to mistrust their mother. They could at least rely on their father to operate according to schedule, adhere to recognizable appearances and disappearances. Their mother, on the other hand, confused and scared them. Sometimes, instead of doing her homework, Eleanor stared at Rita as she sliced a variety of root vegetables and slid them into a crackling pan. She searched for cracks, breakdowns, moments where that black hair might seep through its orange dye.

. . .

The year before Eleanor entered high school was the same year that Narisa was expelled from it. After several infractions of its rules and regulations, the school sent a letter home with Narisa, threatening permanent and immediate expulsion for: twenty-three days of truancy, forty-nine tardies, and an incident in which she was suspected of the possession of marijuana on school grounds, which they could not prove since she was doubly suspected of having eaten the incriminating evidence they had been searching her locker for. The letter recommended careful observation and routine urinalysis to confirm whether or not Narisa was, in fact, a drug user.

It was strange for Narisa to appear at the gate of Eleanor's middle school and offer to walk her home. She hadn't done this in years. Before high school, Narisa had walked home with Eleanor every day. The elementary and middle schools were on adjacent plots of land, three quarters of a mile from their house. The walk home involved two intersections, the first of which was governed by a crossing guard whose metal bracelets jangled at her wrist as she waved the schoolchildren forth.

The second crossing was far enough from the school that there was no demand for a volunteer to guard it. On the other side of this intersection lay a weed-ridden sidewalk, which lined a chain-link fence, which lined the canal, which would lead the girls all the way to their house. A small, jagged opening in the fence could be infiltrated by two sisters if they held their backpacks to their chests and crouched low enough.

The reappearance of this old routine was pleasant, and Eleanor stayed quiet as they walked so as not to break the spell. At the edge of the canal, Narisa slowed and came to a halt. She took the expulsion letter from her backpack and flung it toward the water. It sailed and floated a bit on the breeze before finding its way to the canal's surface.

"Don't narc," she said to Eleanor.

Eleanor shook her head, swore she wouldn't.

The letter was a light white boat on the surface, and the girls waited to watch it sink before they turned and went home.

. . .

For the first several days of her expulsion, neither Jing nor Rita even noticed that their daughter wasn't attending school. Typically, the girls were gone before their parents awoke each morning. Eleanor stayed true to her word and let nothing slip about Narisa's expulsion. But within a few days it no longer mattered. There were district protocols in place in the event that a student did not dutifully bring an administrative letter home to their parents. Phone calls were made, messages were left on answering machines. Letters were mailed to home addresses and parents' places of work.

Narisa and Eleanor were watching TV on the couch in the living room when Mrs. Liu called her oldest daughter to the kitchen. She held the letter up, her hand stiff like a claw. "Come here."

Rita reached into the cabinet above the microwave for the thick, metal ruler. It was dull with rounded edges, which meant it rarely broke skin. But it was heavy. Rita counted out the sixteen strikes in her head, one for each year her daughter had lived under her roof. In middle school, Rita had gotten the ruler, too. Both times administered by Sister Jiang, and both times for wearing her skirt too short. It was palms up for the first offense, knuckles up for the second.

Rita smiled remembering Sister Jiang in her ugly, woolen dress, sweating from the effort and from the thick air of an August afternoon in Taipei. Yes, she smiled, and then she buried that smile, and whatever its accompanying feeling was, as quickly as she could.

Narisa winced but didn't make a sound. When she was a child, she would cry and snivel over the dry slaps against her knuckles, make nonsensical, curse-filled vows of retribution. But now she stood quietly, watching her mother—this small, brittle woman—bring a ruler down with the force of her whole body, as if she were driving a stake into hard ground.

"Ma, come on," Narisa said. "Aren't I too old for this?"

Rita's free hand flew toward her daughter's face, but Narisa was used to this reaction by now and evaded it.

. . .

Eleanor was an uncomplicated girl and a quick, if injudicious, learner. She stippled a self out of little modifications, reactions to what she feared or disliked in the rest of her family. Having never been subject to the metal ruler, Eleanor was afraid of Rita's violences, and it was shortly after witnessing the consequences of Narisa's bad behavior that she became properly motivated to do well in school. (Perhaps Rita would have been happy to know that all her disciplining was not for nothing. That it had percolated elsewhere.)

That winter, Eleanor entered the 2002 Middlesex County Public School Invention Convention. Students grades six through eight across the county were invited to research, design, and build an invention that would improve upon an already-existing product. Think portable cupholder. Think waterproof notebook. With some encouragement from Ms. Paridou, the sixth-grade science teacher, Eleanor filled out two copies of the entrance form and submitted it to the Invention Convention chairwoman, which was Ms. Paridou.

Ms. Paridou often sighed loudly about the types of inventions she wished she had as a teacher, mused even more loudly about what materials might be needed to make these inventions. And Eleanor dutifully pocketed each crumb from this trail, took notes, made lists. They spent a month's worth of lunchtimes together at work on her invention, a series of magnetic school supplies that fit into a magnetic backpack, which meant all objects would stay in place and never go missing.

Sometimes they spent the lunch period in silence, Ms. Paridou reading one of her worn paperbacks and Eleanor reading about magnets at Ms. Paridou's computer, which led her to read about the earth's poles, which led her to read about seafloor spreading, and so on. Ms. Paridou smiled as she printed more articles for Eleanor to read. "It's nice to feed our curiosities, isn't it?"

Rita approved of Eleanor's decision to enter the Invention Convention. In fact, she approved of any competitive activity, as a way for her daughters to set goals in an otherwise easy and overprivileged existence. "Sure, you can eat, go to school, sleep every day. That's a kind of life. No push, never hungry. Look around. People live that way. But then what makes you different from a pig on a farm?"

Sometimes Rita made herself depressed thinking this way. What *did* make her different from a farm animal? Everything she did was erased each day and had to be done again. She cooked, her children ate, and she cooked again. She showered, became dirty, and showered again. She earned money, she spent it, and earned it again. Was this the life she wanted? She tried to recall what she had thought about on that flight (her first) from Taipei to JFK over twenty years ago. What had she wanted then? She couldn't remember. She could hardly remember what it felt like to want at all.

She at least took comfort in her projects. Photographing the trees, the canal, the people of their town. The prints were nothing Rita would call art or artistry—and she certainly never showed them to anyone—but they were evidence of something in her. A part of her that hadn't yet been divvied up and parceled out to the world. Some kernel of the person she had been before.

.   .   .

The weekend before the Invention Convention, Eleanor was nothing more than a small, round head bent over the kitchen table, which was covered by two layers of newsprint. She applied painstaking precision to her project, using a small paintbrush to glue thin magnetic strips to the edges of a series of folders and binders.

"What's this?" Rita asked.

"School supplies, magnetic ones."

"My smart daughter," Rita said. "Will you win? Who are the judges?"

"I don't know. I guess we'll see."

"What was the winner from last year like?"

In fact, Eleanor knew she would not win, because there were no winners. According to MCPS Invention Convention rules, each entry would be scored independently and anonymously, and, regardless of score, each student would receive a detailed critical response and a small medal in the shape of an Erlenmeyer flask.

"Last year's winner was smart," Eleanor said without looking up from her work. She wanted to be left alone now. "Eighth grader, Chinese girl, very pretty." She thought of Narisa and frowned as she tried to summon another face.

"Oh." Her mother was disappointed at this news. She sighed. "Then how is another Chinese girl going to win this year?"

Like most liars, Eleanor's habit of bending the truth had begun as a way to please her mother. Yes, she pleased her mother in the traditional way—by doing what she was asked, by coming when she was called—but Eleanor understood that what pleased Rita most was not the simple completion of tasks; it was to be vindicated, to be assured that what she understood of the world was correct and worth believing. This was why Rita sparred so often with Narisa, who had never learned how to reflect their mother's image back to her because she always sought her own.

Secretly, Eleanor believed them both weak, Narisa and her mother, their constant need for self-assurance, for mirrors everywhere they looked. And it was around this time that Eleanor came to admire her father for the simple fact that she neither pleased nor displeased him. She saw a particular dullness in his eye when he looked at her, the way you look at a brick or a stone, an object you don't expect to move.

6

From: Rita HW Liu <rita.liu21.68@hotmail.com>
Date: Mon, December 4, 2012, 22:47
Subject: I am mad
To: <liueleanr@gmail.com>

Daughter,

I hope you are happy now. You are a mystery from me,
your own mom. Is this what you want? We are all
already mystery from each other. All strangers. Why
hide yourself from me? Why why?

   Mindy Auntie says this is how American children
are. Americans grow up by rebelling and disrespect.
They escape parents and don't come back. Easy for her
to say. She has no child. It is like having no heart.

Every week, my daughter my heart comes to my house. Tell me lies, act like a ghost. Nothing real. Show me pictures of flowers you find on the sidewalk. Coffee mugs you buy online. Handsome men you don't like. Where is my daughter, I think. But I did not say anything. I let you act your way. You think I was never young? Never hide myself because myself was sad, crazy, and alone?

Now you are married. Why? Maybe you love this Ellis. Fine. He is a nice boy. In love, you can kiss. You can have sex. But why marry? To love someone is not a ladder. You don't need to climb to the top. Marriage is serious. It's the end of your own life. The start of another life.

You think you are escaping me? By getting married? Let me tell you the truth. A woman never escape.

·   ·   ·

On Monday, I arrive at Sinai's brutalist campus just after 1:00 p.m., earlier than usual. The air feels colder and wetter in the city than in Matawan. Fall arrived early this year, and though our mice are housed in a windowless, temperature-controlled basement facility, many of their birth rates have already slowed for the cold months ahead.

I'm not in much of a mood to see other people from lab, so I take the stairs directly down to the animal facility, ducking past two grad students I've met before. At the entrance to the mouse room, I hang my bag on a hook by the door and slip on the blue footies, gown, hairnet, and gloves. My principal job right now is to breed and train mice—specific genetic strains with certain neurons that are sensitive to light—for Ellis, Penny, and a few other postdocs.

Of all the racks of mice, Ellis's are closest to the door. I look in at one of his breeders and discover that she's given birth four days ahead of schedule. She's surrounded by nine pups, all licked clean. They are hairless and blind and have soft, pink claws. I lift each pup by its tail to determine its sex. I record the numbers.

Males are returned to their mother where they stumble over each other, feel blindly in front of them. Females are placed in a separate cage (their hormonal cycles affect the data too much). You're supposed to feed a tube through an opening at the top of the second cage and let the carbon dioxide seep through. Watch for movement in their tails, and when there is none, pull each neck from its spine. Protocol is to kill them twice.

Though I've stopped following protocol. I let the male and female pups nurse together, and when they're ready, I wean the females for my own research. I keep my salvaged mice in the unassuming, bottom-most rack, labeled with Ellis's name and other pertinent information about their genetic makeup. Waste not.

After taking care of Ellis's new pups, I check on mine. Six of them are nesting, milling about, scratching at their ears. One is asleep, and I nudge her gently awake. I replace food pellets and refill the water bottle, then return the cage to the low rack. It's a lot of work—this animal husbandry, and I've started developing an allergy to the mice, which appears on my cheeks and waters my eyes.

"Oh, yes," my mother said when I informed her that Ellis had been gracious enough to find work for me in his lab. "Yes, he is doing you some great favor. Work with my animals. All types. Work on my farm." She had always been partial to farm-life metaphors. "How can a man respect you? How can he love you? If you are his inferior?"

"Ma. It's just the way labs work," I said. Admittedly, I hadn't even told her that I'd dropped out of the program. At this point, she was very weak, and part of me genuinely thought another disappointment might hasten her death. A different part of me simply did not want to deal with more of her strident disapproval.

I thought if she just got to know him, she might soften. But when I brought Ellis to her house one afternoon, she only doubled down on her objections. From her bedroom window, we could see him touring the potted ferns on the patio, turning and watering them while we chatted inside. I applied a viscous lotion to my mother's arms and back.

"An American man for you?" she said. "Not a fortuitous match. He'll be too powerful for you."

"Powerful." I laughed. I had never thought to describe Ellis this way.

"What does he want with you exactly?" she said. Then, ducking her head as if to whisper, she spoke at the same volume. "Don't make yourself weak for him. Is that what you're doing?"

"They do have that saying," I said, "about opposites."

"Your jokes," she spat. "My youngest daughter can never be serious anymore. Can never say the truth. This lao mei probably likes that, too. But did you know that you did not laugh, did not smile, for the first seven years of your life? Can an American handle someone so solemn? Someone as serious as you? You are my child. Don't forget that. I knew you from the beginning."

I pushed her gently forward, to rub the balm into her back. There were long red marks, where she had scratched herself. Jiajia had reported unbearable, phantom itches to me.

"Ai," my mother moaned. "Why are you married? Get a divorce." It would become a common refrain via text, call, email in the coming months. "My friend's son just got one. It's easy nowadays. You're too young. Be practical. Trust me."

Trust her. If I were another woman, I might have admired her tenacity. Imagine the determination. Waking up each morning, nearing the end of your life, and still hewing to the one fact you knew to be true: that your daughter was making a mistake. It was all she could talk about when I arrived each Sunday. It was all she could think when I was away (which I knew from the way she bubbled forth with talk of divorce each time I stepped into her house).

The trouble was not even that I disagreed with her. The trouble was that, in the last months of her life, it had become the only thing she wanted to talk about. This refusal of my marriage became her dogma. The daily texts about leaving him were her prayers. And seemingly, I was the lord who would answer them. She waited, she hoped. Is there a more unrequited love than this?

It was the height of summer when she died. Dragonflies mated on the surface of the canal behind the house, touching down on bits of leaves and twigs that floated along the water. Jiajia took pictures of them with her cell phone.

In planning the funeral services, Jiajia seemed to know everything. She insisted that my mother's favorite flowers were calla lilies. Why should I protest that, I thought? That my mother wanted to be buried, not cremated. I certainly had no inkling of her feelings on this matter. That her boyfriend, Tommer, should offer a short speech and prayer at the service. I did not even know my mother had had a boyfriend.

I agreed to all of these fine points. It felt somehow embarrassing and inappropriate to question Jiajia's expertise in the details of my mother's life. In the end, I paid for the stone and the burial but was otherwise uninvolved in planning. After the service, the boyfriend bowed his glossy head and shook my hand. Ellis rested a hand on my shoulder as we walked to the car. Bird shit, red with berries, festooned its roof and hood. Neither my sister nor my father appeared, which was no surprise. They had abandoned us a long time ago, each for their own reason.

7

Upstairs, I sit at my desk and work through my inbox, alternating between answering emails, skimming papers, and reading various articles online. (Part of my job description at the lab is to deliver updates on the latest research in optogenetics to the group every few weeks.) Someone starts rinsing glassware in the large sink directly behind me, and I pretend to read PubMed articles for so long that I begin to actually read them.

At three in the afternoon, white lights flash through the hallways, and an atonal bleating fills the air. People clear the floor at a sluggish, goading pace, the way some pedestrians defy cars to hit them in the crosswalk. Does a fire dare ignite us? I climb the stairs to the seventh floor and find Ellis exactly where I expect him to be, standing over the microscope at his rig.

I shout his name above the alarm. He waves a distracted hand, slouches farther over the eyepiece.

"Ellis!" I shout again. "It's a fire. Let's go."

He curses at the barrel of his microscope.

"There's never a fire," he says, then follows me down the stairs.

. . .

There is a fire. In one of the basement levels where the animal facilities are held. We evacuate to the sidewalk on the south side of 98th Street, where we have plain view of the three fire trucks that arrive in quick succession. Some sense of urgency is missing here, perhaps on account of the slow-moving firefighters. Or the fact that there are no visible flames licking at the walls and windows.

People in scrubs and white coats mill about the sidewalk, having quiet conversations about where the fire is and what the potential damage could be. Ellis runs a hand through his hair repeatedly. I ask him if he should just go ahead and pull out a few strands.

"I'm in the middle of an experiment, and now it might be burnt to a crisp," he says.

Samir emerges from the alley sometime after us. We were in the same cohort together, and now he's one of Ellis's grad students. His T-shirt is wet, darkest at the shoulders, and some soaked strands of hair fall toward his face. In the crook of his elbow, he's holding a pile of notebooks and documents dappled with water.

"What's going on up there?" Ellis asks him.

"Someone rigged the motor of a hairdryer to keep their mice warm instead of using a real heater. It caught fire," Samir says.

"Are you sure that's the reason?" I ask.

"Are you fucking kidding me?" Ellis says at the same time.

Samir doesn't answer me. "Yeah," he says. "It's not too bad. It set off some sprinklers though. They say we'll be back inside within the next few hours."

"What kind of idiot," Ellis says.

Samir: "Probably a first-year, trying to save his PI some money."

Ellis makes a frustrated groan and runs a hand through his hair again. Samir gives me a look, but I pretend not to see.

• • •

By the time we're able to get back into the building, most people, including Ellis, have trickled home or elsewhere. My schedule is largely unaffected, and I simply return to my desk as if nothing has happened. This week, I've been recording my mice while they sleep (from eight o'clock to two in the morning). Under normal circumstances, a person would simply train their mice to sleep during the day so that one could maintain their own schedule for sleeping and working. But I can only use the rigs when they aren't being occupied by more official researchers. And anyway, I prefer recording at night, when I can move about with no concern for what others might think about me, without answering questions about what I'm doing and why.

In the lab's spartan kitchen, I program a coffee, and the machine whirs, clicks, and drips to life. With mug in hand, I make my way toward one of the experiment rooms. Faint brown shoe prints stain the linoleum of the elevator bank and the second-floor hallway. Many of the computers and rigs are in automatic reboot, blinking and requesting logins and passwords.

The door to Ellis's office is open, and I find Samir cross-legged on the floor, combing through a mess of Ellis's water-logged notes. According to the stout building security manager who announced we could return, the second-floor sprinklers were activated for only about ten minutes. One of these sprinklers hangs directly above Ellis's desk like mistletoe, and now his disheveled files, unwashed beakers, zip-locked mice and mouse parts are drenched. Many of his papers are wet and wilted. Handwritten notes have been muddled into blue smudges.

It's partly his fault. One aspect of Ellis's scientific practice is a general snubbing of his nose at the accepted methods for collecting and storing data. He's known (not affectionately) as the cowboy of Mount Sinai's neurobiology department.

Standing there, I offer my help, but Samir declines it. He lays wet sheets of paper flat on the floor. He has one of those haircuts that makes him look like a ballpoint pen. Short fade at the sides, thick and black on top.

"Are you recording overnight again?" he asks. The sleeve of his shirt skims my leg as he reaches for a wire-bound note-book behind me.

I nod. "A few more days and I'll have two full weeks of data."

He doesn't look up from his organizing. A pair of dark blue scrubs rushes past the open door.

"What's all the recording for?" he asks.

"Just personal interest, I guess."

"You know you won't be able to use it, right? Even if you join the program again."

"Oh? It hadn't occurred to me."

"Sorry. I guess you knew that."

"I mean, I'm still interested in the project, just not the program and its pressures."

He nods.

"Are you staying late tonight?" I ask.

"Not too much longer. Just cleaning up now so I don't have to get too involved in it tomorrow."

"This wasn't part of the job description, was it?"

Samir lets a neat stack of papers fall into the metal bin beside him. "So, should we talk about the fire you started?"

"I thought it might be a secret we carry to our graves."

I swear his cheekbones swell into a smile, but it's hard to tell from the angle of his head, and I'm prone to wishful thinking.

8

I head to the basement. For over a week now, I've recorded the offline (sleeping) neuronal activity in the female mice I keep on the low rack of the mouse wall. Before that, I spent many hours training them to complete certain tasks. The first task was simple and easy to replicate: Press a green button, receive food. Press a red button, receive a light shock. The food falls through a wide straw into the mouse's cage. The shock (light but not painless) is administered to the mouse's paws directly from the metal floor of its testing platform.

The tasks, all of which involve spatial navigation, become increasingly complex. Press a button three consecutive times, receive raisins. Press a button two or four times, receive a shock. Follow a marble down its path (a labyrinthian passageway constructed by heavily monitored undergraduates), receive raisins. Follow a marble down its slanted passageway, receive food only if you depart from it at a crucial fork in the tunnel.

Mice learn quickly, they memorize. (This says nothing of their intelligence—though there is a wealth of studies that addresses this particular attribute. It says only that they are properly motivated: starved before running through the experiments. Otherwise, they tend to be lax and easily distracted.)

Having trained in this paradigm for a few weeks, my mice are older and wiser now; their brains are equipped with a taste for raisins, wired for completing a certain unwieldy maze. Now I can compare the baseline recordings of their brain activity prior to learning these tasks to those after they have made memories of running, navigating, eating, suffering shocks.

The question is: What does this mean? How does a mouse "make" a memory? We know that sleep, or even quiet wakefulness, stabilizes memories. But how? Where? Why are memories generated in one area of the brain but then recalled and reactivated in another area? The tasks I present to the mice are memorized over time, but what is "memorize"?

It was while performing the analysis in a previous version of this experiment that I became overwhelmed and left the neuroscience program entirely. I had sifted through hours and hours of activity, analyzed the data for any possible correspondence in timing or across cells, but I couldn't make sense of any of it, couldn't lift a shred of meaning out of it that didn't feel utterly imposed by me.

When I approached Penny about this feeling (of phoniness, artificiality), she knitted her eyebrows so intensely that I knew pity and worry were about to cast their long shadows over everything I said. I cut the meeting short, saying, "Please don't bring up my mother." I remember thinking I should not have cut my own hair the night before.

. . .

Each of my six mice has undergone two surgeries. First, a section of the skull is removed, and a dye is injected into the brain. A glass window is implanted in the skull, covering the exposed tissue. Second, two bolts are inserted at the base of the neck. (By bolting them to the metal posts I've attached to the rig table, I can keep their heads still during recordings.)

Before starting tonight, I check on Samir's surgical work again. I inspect the seams of the windows for tissue degradation or infection, nudge the neck bolts for wiggle room and look for reactions of pain or discomfort. But Samir's work is always flawless. Before joining our lab, he was in ocular research, removing and replacing pupils in mouse eyes, which are about twelve times smaller than their brains. When I first asked him to help me, I voiced my uncertainties about leaving the precision work to him, especially on a project that was essentially unsanctioned.

Samir had laughed. "I think I can handle this clumsy plate you want on their heads." Seeing my face, he added, "I'm good at this. Ask Ellis."

"I don't need to ask Ellis." I was the one who had vouched for him, after all, when Ellis was looking for a graduate student to hire.

"If I botch the surgery, I'll pay for the new mice out of pocket." Samir smoothed his hair, betraying a flair for the theatrical. "Or whatever. It's your call, obviously. Whatever you decide. They're your mice."

That sudden swerve into deference—a hallmark of the son of immigrant parents—was comforting to me. Samir's parents were from Pakistan. They'd arrived in the US the same year that my father had, in 1979. Like me, Samir had been the first in his family to go to college, the first to pursue a graduate degree. Like me, he was not a disappointment exactly, but a deviation from what had been envisioned, dreamt of.

This was a running joke of ours when we first met, something we had in common. Weren't we playing a cruel trick on our parents, whose immigrant longings for the ultimate vision of success, stability, respectability in America translated into a fervent wish that their children become medical doctors? Wasn't a doctorate in the sciences a kind of mockery of that ambition?

Samir liked to joke that it was not disobedience that had led him to neuroscience, but a problem of translation. "If only my dad had said the word 'physician,' things would be different."

As for me, I don't believe my mother ever fully understood the difference. Even by the time of her death, she was still of the belief that I would one day clear a six-figure salary while being valuable to society in the most explicit and unimpeachable way. She thought I was in some more research-heavy version of medical school, and before she died last year, I'd been too mired in other disappointing behaviors to tell her that this wasn't the case.

I attach the first mouse to the rig's table with two headposts. The roll pins needle through the posts and into screw holes on either side of her neck. I offer some food and the tip of a water bottle. She eats and drinks as normally as she can. It takes only a few minutes for her to adjust to the limited movement of her head and neck. (We've been doing the same thing every night for ten days now.) I position the microscope above the cranial window and watch the attached monitor. Neurons prickle and constellate across the screen, thin flashes of fluorescent light across black cells.

The mouse begins to nod off around 8:30 p.m., and another half hour passes before she settles deeper into sleep. I typically record each mouse for about four hours. In that time, I scroll through the day's texts and emails. I read articles and watch video clips. I take walks around the empty corridors. I'm careful not to walk past Ellis's office or the open-plan area of the lab where Samir's desk sits. The other mice doze in their cage. Periodically I eat some of their raisins.

After the first recording is done, I gently unscrew the mouse from her headposts. As I place her back in the cage, I can feel the drowsiness in her body, her faint, expectant breaths. Another mouse takes her place, and the process begins all over again.

In last year's recordings, I stared for hours and came up with nothing. No discernible pattern. No rhyme or rhythm between regions of the brain. I simply watched neurons fire at random, like bolts of Olympian lightning.

What is supposed to be meaningful in any of this? I remember asking Penny. What am I doing here? What is meaningful, and what is a wish for meaning?

9

In the men's bathroom, there's a pilled sofa that Samir and I use to conduct our affairs. At 1:00 a.m., my second mouse is about halfway through its recording session. I hustle Samir onto the thin, foam couch cushions, and he presses a warm hand between my breasts. He kisses me uncertainly. I bite his neck, then that trapezial bit of flesh. His hands move along my body and toward my legs, as if divining something precious and geodic beneath the flesh.

He kneels between my legs, and I watch the pale, hypnotic spot at the crown of his head—no larger than a dime—track the movement of his mouth.

We lie there for a while afterward, chatting and joking. We stifle giggles when we hear someone try the door that we've locked. At 3:30 a.m., I return to my mice, and Samir returns to whatever he's working on. We don't ask each other what we're busy with, lest we goad each other into revealing (or having to pretend) that we're only here for each other.

The sky is edging into a seamless pink when I arrive at home. The air is wet. Birds trill and jurry from the branches of the low oak in front of our house.

.   .   .

When we were very young, my mother (thirty-six) and I (seven) shared a joke in which she accused me of reading too many stories.

"Where do you find these things?" she would say while I sat absorbed in the books she herself had bought and paid for at the store.

"How do you have the time for this?" she'd joke as she drove me to and from the library.

She had a low, airy laugh, which rippled through her nose. I mimicked it, which sometimes made her tilt her head back in even more laughter, like a Pez dispenser.

Eventually, this joke lost its luster. She did begin to wonder where I found the books she hadn't paid for. How I still had so much time for them. I did pay more attention to words on pages than, for example, my face in the mirror. I spent more time reading books than reading social cues from, say, potential friends or boyfriends.

One evening, she knocked on the door of my bedroom. She did not enter, only stood on the threshold, one hand on the knob.

"You can fill your head with this nonsense for now," she said. "But it will only become more and more difficult to pour it all out again."

Here is the mark of a person who has read too many stories: We think excitement ought to beget more excitement. We think action will outdo itself with more action, that each explosion of great and singular activity will be followed by yet another, even greater one. This is not how nature works, of course. In nature, a period of great activity is followed always by a period of stillness, an interval in which dormancy and death are indistinguishable to the naked eye. Think of the calm before a storm. Think of the calm after.

One Scholar Is Enough

The Invention Convention turned out to be an event of great indignity. Eleanor had been obsessed with the actual creation of the prototype: a series of magnetic folders, pens, and pencils that attached themselves to corresponding magnets sewn into the lining of a backpack. But she understood now that what mattered was not the precision or functionality of the prototype, but the ambition of the project.

Students across Middlesex County had dreamt up solar-powered hover boards, self-washing clothes, a productivity desk that chirped if your head was drooping too close to its surface.

"You glued magnets to some pencils," said Noush, a peer reviewer for the Invention Convention projects. She was a volunteer—an older girl with thinned-out eyebrows and hair you could swim in.

Eleanor mentioned the more interesting facts about magnets to her. That the earth was a magnet. Did Noush know? That each year the oceans spread by several inches because large plates of earth moved apart, making way for new crust to emerge from beneath the surface. That every so often the new crust would reverse polarity (since the earth's core itself periodically reversed its magnetic polarity), which resulted in a symmetrically striped ocean floor along both sides of the spread. Eleanor pointed at an image of the stripes, which she'd glued to her board.

"I'll make a note," Noush said. "A ton of pointless research."

Ms. Paridou, who had sanctioned this embarrassing research, was nowhere to be found.

For participating, Eleanor received a brass-colored pendant in the shape of a miniature Erlenmeyer flask that dangled from a short, green ribbon. She pinned it to her shirt for the rest of the school day (and suffered teasing for doing so). At home, she told her parents that she'd won second place. Narisa snorted. "I guess they changed the rules since I was there," she said.

*   *   *

Eleanor wrapped the role of house scholar around herself like a heavy, protective coat. She began to spend long, quiet hours in her room. So busy with her studies was she that

Rita exempted her from washing dishes and putting place-mats and leftovers away. Her chores evaporated. Things were peaceful, and no one bothered her.

Within a few weeks, Eleanor developed reading headaches and eye strain, which Rita suspected were psychosomatic but which she indulged nonetheless with cold compresses and kudzu root tea. (Scholars were sensitive people, were they not? Neither Rita nor Jing had been particularly gifted at school, but they'd had a neighbor who was. Rita and her friends made fun of his pallor, his sunken eyes. "What's the point of being smart if you're all but dead?" her friend Jewel had said once. But he'd gotten the highest examination score in the neighborhood and then gone to university at Tai Da. Some things were as simple as that.)

In fact, Eleanor was not that bright a student. She had a good memory and an inclination for following directions, but aside from this, she was not an exceptional or even very capable thinker. Literature did not touch her. History was an exertion of pure memory. Though her grades were good, she was never a standout among students; too shy to be called charming, too careful to be considered gifted.

Eleanor was simply quiet and could be for long periods of time. And this was what Rita envisioned a modern scholar to be: someone actively engaged in disappearing, in self-effacing, someone hermited within themselves. Perhaps Rita was envisioning those ancient, Daoist recluses—poets, scholars, intellectuals, elders—who retreated into the mountains and did not draw attention to themselves. Rejected fame, fortune, reputation, and instead sought detachment, solitude, enlightenment. (How many of these scholars were not recluses but political exiles, banished at the whims of dynastic turnover and ruler favor? This was not the sort of question Rita was inclined to ask.)

It didn't occur to Rita to wonder why Eleanor never corrected mistakes, never offered opinions, convictions, suggestions, clarifications. Never revealed anything about what she knew or did not know, what she felt or did not feel. How had she trained herself to be so amenable? Where did she learn to nod at concepts she didn't understand? Simple. Eleanor did not really rule herself or any realm of her life. She inhabited a world that belonged always to someone else.

.   .   .

Of the weed-smoking teens in Sayreville High's class of 2003, only Narisa had been expelled. Jared was delivered a one-week suspension after his father revitalized the music and arts program with an anonymous $1,500 donation. Lily served eight Saturday detentions—her mother, an unverified PhD in economics, offered to head the school-wide "Boom and Crash" stock market simulation that spring. CJ, whose father was dead and whose mother struggled to support her two sons while managing a barbecue restaurant, perhaps knew that he had no leverage. He had all along been storing his weed in Narisa's locker, only, he claimed, because it was closest to the parking lot.

Jing and Rita were not aware of these arrangements, or the myriad ways one could save one's child from expulsion had you the proper resources. Though they had the money (it surprised their nosier neighbors the brands of cars and home furnishings a business in wigs and dollar-store hair accessories could afford), they hadn't the knowledge nor the audacity to approach someone as esteemed as the county superintendent with something even remotely resembling a bribe. Rita thought that America was exceptional in its purity, its incorruptibility. Jing, on the other hand, was under no illusion that American officials were incorrupt or incorruptible; he merely understood that they were not corruptible by someone like him.

There was an expulsion hearing, a chance for Narisa to make some sort of last-ditch plea. But, for reasons that would only make sense to a teenager, she failed to appear. She disappeared for three days, during which Rita stalked about the house like a starved predator, and Eleanor and her father both kept to themselves. When she came home, she took a long, luxuriant shower, which Rita interrupted by throwing the door open and shutting off the water. Rita was startled briefly by Narisa's childish body. Thin, bony shoulders. Small pointed nipples floating on shapeless, flat breasts. This girl was hers?

"Enough. Get out." She grabbed Narisa by a fistful of thick wet hair. "You waste my water."

So Narisa packed her things (clothes, toothbrush, MP3 player) and moved them and herself to the second floor of her father's warehouse.

Jing and Rita themselves had occupied the second floor when they'd first acquired the place. Now the space was separated by slapdash drywall into a kitchen area, a serviceable bathroom, and two sizable rooms. In recent years, it had come to serve as living quarters for workers who could not risk the requisite checks for more formal rental arrangements. (Many of the workers had neither credit nor background to speak of.) The rooms were sporadically occupied—meant to be used as a temporary solution until workers found better arrangements with friends or had saved enough cash to obviate the need for a credit check.

"Occupied," Jing said as he led Narisa past the larger of the two rooms. Narisa nodded at its closed door, to which clung a red upside-down cutout of the character for "fortune."

The smaller room was sparsely furnished with a wireframe cot and a green card table. Its previous occupant was a young man from Wuhan who had left for Chinese New Year celebrations early that month and never returned.

"Maybe he hated it here," Narisa said, testing the air with the tendrils of her foul mood, "and didn't want to tell you."

"It may be," Jing said. But the boy had left wrinkled clothes and linens hanging to dry on cables pulled across the room. A black, laminated bible sat on a table that was also home to several of the same wooden combs, carved with lotus flowers and flat peaches. This wasn't the room of someone who had made plans not to return.

"Clean it out," Jing said. "Keep whatever you want. Throw the rest away."

Narisa swept a molding orange into the trash, then fit her bike into a narrow space by the door.

. . .

It was perfectly acceptable to Jing that Narisa would join him at the warehouse. They had Eleanor, didn't they? One scholar in the family was enough. Narisa would learn the family business, and in some near or distant future, she would take over his responsibilities. The thought of such a takeover filled Jing with a profound sense of relief, and the subsequent thought that it would be so many years before this transition happened exhausted him. Was life really so long?

At the warehouse, Narisa dusted shelves, stacked boxes, swept beads and fabric from the cutting floor. On busier days, she sat with the workers who were inundated with bright ribbon bows to glue to metal clips, or tubs of faux pearls to thread onto black elastic bands.

Briefly, she fantasized about her guidance counselor or some other interested party knocking on the door, threatening her parents with a truancy lawsuit. But no one appeared. No one looked for her. Not even her friends. It occurred to Narisa just how tenuous your ties to the world could be. It was the first time she'd understood that there was no one holding on but you. That if you strayed far enough, the gravitational pull dwindled away. You could just float off and disappear.

"Is she spying on us or something?" Minru muttered to Peng. They sat on one side of an oblong table. Minru threaded pink beads onto brown leathered fringes, Floriana tied them up in bows, Peng glued them to plastic clips.

Peng chuckled through his nose, but he kept his eyes trained on the glue gun. He was determined not to be distracted by these other workers. Lazy, slow, ill-mannered. His fingers worked nimbly. He was on his sixty-seventh leather bow that morning.

. . .

Peng and his daughter, Jiajia, were the occupants of the second room upstairs. They had arrived at the entrance of the warehouse last December. At the door the father and daughter had collected themselves. Peng brushed flecks of snow from his daughter's hair. Jiajia tugged at the wet, puckered collar of her father's shirt. They tried the door, and it was unlocked, but Peng thought it best to remain respectfully at the entrance of Liu Enterprises. Jiajia's cheeks were pink from the cold. Beyond the building, tall skeletal trees shuddered in the wind.

"Hallo," he shouted. And then in Mandarin: "I'm looking for the boss, Liu Jing."

When no one answered, he called again: "Hallo! Lao ban! Brother!"

Eventually, a woman opened the door and peered through it. She looked at the father and daughter, with their massive black suitcase and two stained duffel bags. "Yes? Can I help you?" she said in English.

Peng had prepared for this sentence, and now enunciated it as best as he could, "Ai em heah to se Mista Jing Liu."

Peng and Jiajia were led across the dim warehouse to an even dimmer office that smelled of mold and whiffs of a lunch heavy on chives and garlic. Jiajia yearned for her own bowl of something spicy and piping hot, something that would clear her nose and make her sweat. Earlier, in the airport, they had purchased a meal of puzzling, cold layers: slices of pink, fall-apart meat between slices of chewy bread.

"Brother," Peng said when he saw him. Jing was seated at a wide faux-mahogany desk. A small unpopulated fish tank sat behind him. Beside it, a haphazard box of samples: fashion belts, feathered headbands, scented school supplies, clothes for small dogs.

Jing stood. His gray cotton shirt revealed him to be a careless eater; string-like stains adorned the area just below the chest. Jiajia stared at these as her father introduced himself and her.

"Brother," Peng said. A smile broke across his face. "Brother," he said mistily. "Do you know who we are? Do you not recognize your own face in mine?"

Jing computed the man in front of him. Their resemblance was unmistakable. The same tall nose, flat ears, wide, eclipsed eyes. Still, he remained distant and polite. He collected sample ribbons and fabrics from a folding chair and brushed invisible remnants away.

"Come in," Jing said to the man and his daughter. "Sit down and tell me."

. . .

Peng had been separated from his parents in 1948 during the Chinese Civil War (though, like many separated families, they would not understand that they had been permanently divided until years later). His mother and father had boarded a naval ship to Taiwan without him, leaving Peng behind with his grandparents. They hadn't wanted to disrupt his education and planned to return to collect him within the year. He had been in the first grade.

But they did not return and did not send for him. The following year, all communications between Taiwan and China were banned. Peng's father could occasionally finagle money and letters to his parents by way of messengers in Hong Kong, but he worried that he might mark them as Nationalist sympathizers in a country under Communist control.

Forty years passed before tentative lines of communication between Taiwan and China opened again. In that time, Peng's parents had had three more children, all born in the military dependents' village in Taipei where the family had settled.

"I traveled to Da'an and found Mother's apartment," Peng said. "But it was occupied by someone else. A young man. He called himself a friend of hers." Peng gave a shrug of neither belief nor disbelief.

"She passed away years ago," Jing replied.

Peng nodded mildly. "Her good neighbors told me to find you here."

Jing measured the man before him. He was horribly thin, as if some constant, extraneous energy ran the flesh off his body. The skin at his throat seemed to cleave directly to ligament and bone.

"I bring a photograph," Peng said, "as proof."

"And the letters? From our father."

"They were discovered," Peng said. "We suffered for them."

Jing squinted at the blurry, black-and-white image. Yes, that was his father, wasn't it, holding the hand of a thin, glowering boy? What a stretch from the man who stood here now, smiling, obsequious in his desperation.

"My daughter," Peng started, as if the idea of her had just occurred to him. He motioned at the flat-nosed girl beside him. "She's the reason I am here, Di di. So far from our lao jia. Surely you can understand that." The tendons in his neck pulsed as he spoke of Jiajia, an American life for her. The girl seemed not to notice she was being talked about. She ran her fleshy palms along the leathered piping of their grease-stained suitcase.

"A livelihood, a chance," Peng said. "I beg you, brother. We've come all this way."

. . .

Jing granted Peng a job on the warehouse floor, as he tried always to do for the men and women who came to his door with expired visas or, somehow (he did not press), no visas at all. There was a large, empty room being used for storage on the second floor, and Jing removed the boxes, chairs, desks, and sewing machines. He offered Peng and Jiajia the room upstairs and would not charge them rent for the first three months.

That night, Rita would ask if Jing had lost his will or his mind. "Where is the proof?" Rita insisted. "He looks like you? Ai, you have lived here too long. You think every Eastern man looks like you. Chinese, Korean, Japanese." And the photograph. Was Jing certain it was his father? Why wasn't his mother in the photograph? What if they shared the same father, but not the same mother?

Jing shrugged these questions away. There was the possibility, of course, that it was a scam. That they shared no relation at all, and that Jing was the naive, American mark of a scheming father-daughter duo from the mainland.

Brother, half brother, not-brother. Who cared? These migrants had such small designs. To eat, to live, to lie down on a bed. Was it a scam to ask for a day's work and cash wages? To live and die in America? It was the inexorable dream that had afflicted so many of his own nights in Taipei, where he lay awake listening to the relentless trill of cicada songs. Where he envisioned flat, dry lands peopled by broad-chested blondes with big teeth.

Jing stepped onto the porch outside, and his wife did not follow. A sliver of white light appeared and disappeared as clouds flew past on a high wind. He picked at his teeth with a little wooden rod.

What had he dreamt of before dreaming of America, or some version of it? He both could and could not remember. It was the same feeling he got whenever Rita told the story of his fractured tailbone to their friends. In 1981, he had slipped on a slick of ice that had collected underneath his car. The way she told it, Jing had just lain there and not gotten up. She saw him from the big bay window that looked out onto the yard and driveway. When she ran outside, he remained unmoving, almost underneath the car. She hurried toward him, goose-stepping in her slippers on the glossy iced pavement.

When she got there, Jing stared up at her from the ground. He had the dazed look of a man who has just seen an explosion or a birth. For a month, Rita massaged him, brewed beef broth and fish fins. Never was he so tender with anyone as he was with his own injured ass, she said, at which point Ah Mao or Mindy or whoever would howl with laughter.

Jing would laugh along or avert his eyes, shake his head in jocular protest. But really he couldn't remember this event at all. Not just the fall but the whole month of limping and self-pity. He did recognize himself in Rita's storytelling. He could even visualize himself in Rita's telling, but he didn't have his own version. That memory was gone, as were so many others.

What did he used to love? What did he used to think about? What was Jing like before he had been shaped, like so many others, into an arrow trained on a life of prosperity in America?

What had he hoped for before it was America? Rain. He remembered wishing, in those humid summers, for rain and a cool breeze to part the air.

The Early Days

Rita and Jing had grown up in neighboring military villages in the Neihu district of Taipei. The villages were meant to be provisional housing for KMT military forces and their families in retreat from civil war in China. Each family lived in one standard unit in a long row of identical concrete-walled homes. These were thatched with straw roofs reinforced later by government-issued sheets of corrugated polycarbonate.

Jing and his younger brother were known in the village as indolent, unschoolable boys. They stole watermelons from neighborhood farm plots and threw them in the lake. They offered soup bones to stray dogs but kicked at their ribs if they got too close.

It was a surprise to all when Jing graduated (though at the bottom of his class) from high school, and it was cause for wild speculation when, years later, news traveled along the village's long, gray rows that Jing's mother was borrowing money from the neighborhood hui to send her oldest son to America.

News traveled quickly among the families of this complex. They patronized the same doctors, seamstresses, fruit sellers, fishmongers. They rode the same bus that ferried them to the city's center. The families buzzed with excitement, maledictions, wishes well, lunar auspice suggestions.

Everyone had their take on the matter:

"If I were his mom, I'd rid myself of him, too."

"He'll be a philanderer and a drunk, like his father. Here, anywhere."

"That's the kind of boy who thrives in America. Half ruthless, half imbecile."

Rita, or Huiwen as she was called then, did not partake in the gossip, but she followed it closely. She and her mother sewed, sold, and rented formal dresses to women in the village who could afford them, and they often heard bits and pieces of rumors which they pretended not to hear or care about. Later, they mapped the tidbits together over their sewing patterns.

"Wu Ayi says he's gotten into an exchange program."

"Ha! Lies. What university wants a boy like that for their exchange program?"

"How would you know what a university likes?"

"If that naughty boy goes to an American university, it means anyone can go. I'll sign you up next."

"He was bad as a child, but not anymore."

"He's the same child he was. You're just blinded now by his handsomeness."

"Absolutely not."

"Round eyes, chiseled jaw. I've seen how you get when he's around, little friend."

"Ts, you haven't seen anything."

"I don't hear any talk of Jing getting married. Do you?"

"You've made it your business?"

"Well, he ought to marry someone before he goes."

"I don't think he wants anyone."

"Who he wants is irrelevant. What matters is who wants *him*."

"Eh? Don't look at me like that."

"Why try to throw me off the scent? I know your feelings."

"I don't have any feelings."

"Huiwen, if you don't plant seeds in the garden, what can you expect to grow?"

"A man likes to give chase. You taught me that."

"How can Jing chase what he doesn't know exists?"

"I've made my desires clear to him."

"Yaa. This girl thinks she makes anything clear?"

◆　◆　◆

Later that night, Huiwen waited near the well in the shadow of a diseased maple. She knew Jing to be a man of routine, just off the cusp of his military service. Every evening at nine, perhaps to avoid the rush of young mothers in the morning, he pulled water from the well and sat on the cold stone bench to smoke a cigarette.

Right on time, Jing approached. She watched as he leaned on the pump, as water sloshed and rang into the first metal pail and then the second. Her stomach churned with nerves. Jing bent to lift the pails, lumbered just past her. One of the maple's dipping branches touched the top of his head.

"You should take me with you, Liu Jing," Huiwen said.

Water startled out of their pails, and Jing set them down on the gray dirt.

He looked at the dark figure, shaded from the moon. "Huiwen," he said.

"Think about it." Her own voice energized her, as it would her whole life. She was both snake and charmer. "If you have a wife, she'll be able to take care of you."

"If I have a wife, I'll have to take care of her." A breeze blew east. Moonlight winked on the water that remained in the well basin.

He said goodnight rather stiffly, so as not to encourage her. But there she was the next night.

"What if I leave you alone, Jing? The minute we arrive. We'll say goodbye and never see each other again."

Every evening that Jing returned to the well, Huiwen was there, bargaining, convincing, pleading. There was no elegance or coyness in her bid for Jing's attention. She and her mother were known as shameless, unrelenting saleswomen.

They walked brides-to-be home from the college; they invited recent widows to long afternoons of tea and desserts, where sample fabrics happened to be draped across armoires and the backs of tall chairs.

"I have friends all over," Huiwen said. "Niuyue, Luoshanji, Boshidun. I wouldn't need you. We'll have our own secret agreement. We don't have to tell our parents a thing."

These were the least romantic moonlit rendezvous that Jing had ever heard of.

"So go on your own. What do you need to marry me for?"

"No money, no husband. You think they'll let a woman like me into America? I'm like a cockroach to them. Destined to multiply. It's not so easy for a woman to move around without a man."

A frog belched in the grass. Jing swatted at his neck, tickled by gnats and bold mosquitoes. Sweat formed along his hairline. A native dog trotted past, soup bone jutting from the grip of its teeth. Black fur, pert ears, deep, black-lined eyes. It gave Jing and Rita a wide, suspicious berth.

"Do you think there are stray dogs like this in America?" Jing asked.

"These lazy things? I've never seen them do anything but sleep in the sun and eat what we throw at them."

"They're very loyal, you know. And smart. That's how they stay alive."

"They're alive because we don't have the heart to kill them," she said.

Huiwen glanced behind her at the yellow light coming from the window of her house. It flickered as her brothers moved across one of the rooms upstairs. Huiwen was the oldest of five siblings. Her younger sister, Huifen, was already engaged, and while Huiwen was mildly happy for her sister, who at such an early age seemed already so contented, she also knew what was coming to old, unmarried her. If she didn't act soon, she would be the one who stayed, who took care of the younger ones until they were old enough to fly, who took care of her parents until they flew even further.

"I don't even want to go," Jing said suddenly, interrupting Huiwen's thoughts.

Huiwen laughed, but when she saw Jing's brow darken, she said tenderly, "Life isn't about what we want. It's about our destiny."

It was her canned response to girls who didn't want to get married, women who didn't want to mourn their husbands. They had to face the music, and they might as well wear a fine, hand-sewn dress while doing it.

"All I need is a man for the journey, for my papers," said Huiwen. "Once we've arrived, I'll disappear. You understand. I can take care of myself, as you have seen. Please, Jing."

. . .

After that evening, Jing delegated the task of water-fetching to his younger brother. Ah Mao jumped at the opportunity, as he did with all opportunities that might get him out of the house for a cigarette and a turn about the neighborhood.

"Huiwen was out there again tonight," he said the next week as he watched Jing pack his things for New York.

Jing looked out onto the square that lay between their house and Huiwen's. He couldn't see into the Li house from that angle, but he could picture her as if she were standing in the room between them. Sharp, angular shoulders, a deep line that spanned the very center of her forehead.

"She asked me to marry her," Jing said.

Ah Mao grunted in surprise and amusement.

"So that she can come to America with me."

"She's living in the past." Ah Mao wrinkled his nose. "What Chinese woman still needs to be married to move anywhere she wants? Look at Yeh Mingfang and her television school in Los Angeles. And the Yang twins headed to New York for computer programming."

Jing said nothing, caught a stack of letters and notes as it slid toward the sloping edge of the bed.

"Well, what did you say?"

"I said no."

Ah Mao sucked at his teeth. "Why, ah? You think you'll find an American wife? A woman with big blonde hair who wants a Chinese importer with a big head for a husband?"

Jing parceled out a laugh. "Ya, who knows what the blonde women will want?"

. . .

In preparation for Jing's farewell party, Huiwen and her mother sun-dried pork sausages by the fence that bordered the main road. Her mother accused her of not being direct enough. But what was Huiwen supposed to do? Strip off all her clothes? Climb on top of him in the night? Perhaps someone lewd would appreciate this, like the builder's son. Or Jing's younger brother. But Jing was a more reserved sort. Anything so brash would scare him away.

So Huiwen kept her distance. When she happened to run into Jing at the butcher's stall, she wished him well. When they crossed each other in line at the almond tofu cart, she offered to pray for him during his flight. If he wanted her, he would call to her, she thought. She must not circumvent the burden of waiting. She must exercise patience.

Huiwen attended Jing's farewell gathering in the auxiliary courtyard. She had packed a few pears and some of the sausages in thick paper. She stayed long enough to hand him the package, name its contents.

"You're making a mistake," she said playfully, though the tip of her nose burned. "I won't be here when you come back."

Jing thanked her for the gift. "Maybe I won't come back."

. . .

Jing stayed in Queens, with his oldest sister and her husband, an impatient, pink-nosed man named Hong. It was a busy street, sunlit in the afternoons, lined with gray cinderblock houses with tall, narrow windows through which Jing could glimpse Christmas trees, dining room tables, family photos arranged on the walls. The rotted telephone pole in front of Hong and Mindy's house hosted a basketball hoop made from a plastic crate nailed to a plywood board. During the day, truant children played at it, letting their ball hit the cars that dared to park beneath it. They were beautiful snub-nosed boys. Dominican, Korean, Chinese.

If Hong was home when they played, he shooed them away, called them dogs and demons, threatened to sic the police on them. Unsurprisingly, globules of spit and the stench of urine appeared at the front steps of the house. Errant basketballs seemed always to bounce against the door, followed by cackles and defiant, erect fingers.

"Why," Jing asked, "does he invite their anger?"

"He's not that bad." Mindy waved him away. "Better than a man who just rolls over and lets these little ghosts do as they please." She went on, "Though they seem to do what they please either way. Like you as a child."

He looked at these desperate, frenzied children. Like him? They sang, they laughed, they sometimes screamed at the sky as if they hoped to pierce it. One boy grabbed at the tree branches, ripped them bare of brittle leaves. Another bounced on the hood of a car, checking beneath his seat for a dent in the metal. They howled with laughter if an alarm went off. Later in the afternoons, they disappeared.

Mindy called Jing's name, which snapped him to attention. "Your job isn't to worry about the block's ghosts and hoodlums. Your job is to send the money back."

With one swift movement, Mindy pulled the couch flat, then spread a pilled rosebud-patterned sheet onto its surface. This would be Jing's bed for the next two years.

Bolder by the Day

Winds blew constantly that fall, and the first time Jing saw flurries falling onto the street, he mistook them for ashes. He looked wildly about for the source, the fire, only to see a small red-haired boy staring at him. Strange-looking child, he thought.

Jing let the snow touch his face, the lids of his eyes. Briefly he wished for a fire, but then chastised himself. He did not want anything to burn, he knew. He simply wanted to go home.

At Mindy and Hong's, Jing did his best to keep to himself in the small apartment. Every morning, before Mindy and Hong emerged from their room, he refolded the couch into its daytime configuration and packed his clothes, books, and belongings back into his valise. Then he tucked the thing into the hall closet, where coats the size of burden animals hung in wait. He washed each dish immediately after he used it, chewing the final bite of the meal as he carried his bowl and chopsticks to the sink.

At Mindy's insistence, he ate eggs and porridge and drank tea with her and Hong each morning. In silence, they shared and traded sections of the newspaper, using ads as a makeshift plate for bones, shells, tea leaves, and other breakfast refuse.

After breakfast, Jing and Hong rode the bus together into Manhattan, where Hong conducted his own business and sent his brother-in-law off to meet some of the shop owners, buyers, importers, and purveyors he knew. To these potential customers, Jing presented the samples he had brought with him from Taiwan, a motley collection of umbrellas, faux leather belts, nail scissors, costume earrings for young girls, silvery hair clips, plastic pencil cases, a selection of Huiwen's mother's dresses.

Enterprising friends and neighbors in Taiwan had begged Jing to take their samples with him, hoping that he might sell their products in America. Whatever the Americans wanted, he and his neighbors would provide. Everyone in the world knew Americans spent frivolously. He simply needed to ascertain what it was these people wanted, what motivated them to spend their money.

Hong's acquaintances were polite and generally welcoming, but ultimately none of them wanted anything that Jing had to offer. After a few weeks of these rejections, an Iranian store owner took pity on him. She saw the city's fine dark grime clinging to the sweat on his forehead. She invited him in for some cool water from the tap, some almonds from a bone-colored bowl. A fan circulated the stale air from wall to wall.

"It's not easy," she nodded, as Jing drained the glass. She poured him another. She looked at his things, which he had been careful to keep in sealed bags, lest he stain them with the sweat from his hands or the soot that seemed to float in the New York air.

"Here, child." (He was twenty-four, but he looked obediently at the map she'd dug from a desk drawer that housed sundry papers, wrappers, and uncapped pens.)

"That's where you sell your things." She pointed at Mott Street, which ran perfectly along a crease in the aged map. "Trust me." She pointed at him and drew her finger along the loose border of Chinatown. "Go to your people. I did the same thing you are doing. In America, this is how you start. With your own. With people who will be kind to you."

. . .

When he arrived in Chinatown, Jing ate first. He entered a small noodle shop that smelled of cigarette smoke and stale oil. He sat near the door, and every once in a while, there was reprieve from the heavy smoke and humid kitchen air within. A funeral procession passed by the restaurant, and a dazed-looking woman in a silken white suit shuffled down the slope of the road. On each of her arms was a man in a suit wearing thin-rimmed sunglasses. Trailing them was a black Cadillac, glossy as if it had recently emerged from the sea.

Farther up the street, Jing could see a market across the way. Chopsticks, cleaning supplies, slippers of every color glimmered in the sun. On display in the window were suitcases, backpacks, ties in boxes, light bulbs, gimmick phones, stuffed animals, T-shirts, costume wigs. Two girls played in front, throwing rocks and small plastic figurines at each other. They shouted an impossible pidgin of Cantonese and English. A young man—about Jing's age—sat in a small spot of sunlight, inspecting a stain on the sleeve of his coat.

Jing ordered from his waiter, a thin, slouched boy whose face was marked with red pustules. Almost immediately, a plate of changfen wobbling in a pool of brown sauce landed on his table. Thin slices of scallion and kernels of corn lay on top. "Four bucks," the boy said and waited for Jing to produce the bills from his wallet.

"Four US dollars? Wah, this must be the freshest, best tasting noodle place in New York."

The boy waited.

"Here, have it." Jing put the bills on the table. "For my countrymen, right?"

After, Jing introduced himself to the sunning young man at the market across the way and pointed at the objects he could sell to him for cheaper. Sunglasses, umbrellas, back-to-school pencil kits.

"I get boss," the boy said in English.

A woman with stiff, gray hair and cloudy eyes emerged. Jing repeated his claims about the products that lined the sidewalk in front of the store.

The woman gave him a loud guffaw. She waved Jing away with a smile. "You newcomers. Bolder by the day!" She reorganized the pens and magnets by the register. "You know, in America, you can't just be bold. You have to be smart. You have to know who you're selling to."

"Who am I selling to?"

"An old grandmother. Ha ha! An established shop owner." She returned to stacking bags of dried herbs and beans on a flimsy shelf.

"You don't think every nephew, niece, cousin, son-in-law, daughter-in-law has something to sell me? You don't think everything in this store is what keeps my family working in Hong Kong, what keeps them fed and alive?" She shook her head. "Why would I buy from you? Who am I helping? A handsome stranger from Taiwan?"

. . .

On the 4:46 back to Elmhurst, Hong rolled his eyes. "Chinatown? What were you doing there, ah? Homesick already?"

In hand, Hong had two contracts: 260 umbrellas (160 black, 100 navy blue) and 300 headbands (pink, purple, and navy blue with white polka dots).

"Do you go to a starving man and ask for a bite of his food? Do you go to a poor man and beg him for change?" Hong barked a laugh. "The Chinese here don't have money to spend. Understand? They only have products to sell, or blood and sweat to give away. Just like us, see? The best we can do is leave each other alone. That's how we help each other."

"You were no help," Jing muttered.

"Help yourself!" Hong tapped the left side of Jing's head. "No one wants to see two Chinese men walk into their store with our ugly briefcases, smelling like garlic, sweating from the bus ride. One lonely Chinese man is all they can bear."

Jing looked out onto the East River as their bus lurched and gasped down the boulevard.

Hong went on. "The only people who have money to spend in this country are lao mei. They are buying. Everyone else is selling. Working. If you want to see Chinese people, go home. If you want to make money, you must see only Americans. You must talk like them and smile all the time. You must say please for everything. And thank you."

Jing sneered to show his top row of teeth. He held both thumbs up toward the ceiling of the bus. "A-okay, buddy," he said.

Hong grunted. "This Jing. He understands now, eh? He might start his business after all."

.   .   .

But Jing could not start his business. Within a month, it became clear that he did not know the first thing about selling the wares he had brought with him from Taiwan. At trade shows, which Hong promised would be like catching turtles in a jar, buyers seemed to see right through Jing. His prices were either too high (an affront) or too low (a scam).

"Is it your eyes or something?" Hong whispered to him. They sat at their designated table at the expo center, arrayed with sample products and Hong's costume jewelry and high-gloss pamphlets he'd printed the year before.

"Ta ma de," Hong said. "Smile bigger."

When buyers approached, Hong talked endlessly about his brother's ethical factories in Tainan City, their high standards and quality assurance, all of which translated into products based off European and Japanese design but created and made in affordable, down-to-earth Taiwan. He cooed about wanting to bring East and West together. European ideas and Asian work ethic. Was there a more beautiful marriage than this? He offered his card to buyers (with both hands to connote respect), bowed, and smiled as they moved away.

"It's not that Americans are naive," Hong explained to Jing. "It's that being skeptical takes too much time. Being skeptical has a price. Americans are a people of ideas. And people of ideas are willing to spend money to keep their minds free, at peace."

A man with smoke-colored eyes and a broad-brimmed hat approached. He lingered on Hong's costume jewelry.

"This man," Hong said quietly. "Not American. He's used to marketplaces, hawkers and shouters and wheedlers. Like we are."

Hong handed the man a booklet, then turned back to Jing and continued. "This is a man who appreciates silence, though it may catch him off guard. That is the best position to put your buyer in. They feel respected but confused."

For a while, the two sellers were quiet as the man rubbed the pink stones in a pair of gold-plated earrings. Then, he tipped the booklet toward his head, as if saluting them, and walked away.

"Was he supposed to buy something," Jing said, "because we ignored him?"

Hong grunted. "Those Hassans never buy anything."

.   .   .

Jing was not the pursuant type. In fact, he was rather stand-offish for a man selling ten-use umbrellas and neon fashion belts. For the remaining hours at the trade show, he watched buyers pass him by without saying a word. Or pick up his items and inspect them like ripe fruits, only to put them down again.

As Hong suggested, Jing made note of the presence or absence of wedding rings, the scuff or shine of their shoes. In the pouches beneath their eyes, he saw whether they lacked sleep or sobriety. He guessed at their ages—though lao mei skin always looked so delicate and weathered, it was hard to tell.

"Ta ma de. What am I supposed to do with the information I'm gathering?"

"You blockhead. If you see an older woman showing lots of chest and arms, you know how to talk to her. If you see a young guy with shiny shoes and a Gucci belt, you know how to talk to him."

"I don't think I do," Jing started to say, but Hong had begun a conversation with another buyer. A pouched belly, dark depressions under her eyes, and thin brass-colored hair. Hong moved behind his table, as the woman moved in front of it. He explained each object that entered her line of sight. Here was a delicate silver-plated necklace. Here were chunky, faux turquoise bracelets—very trendy. Any name could be engraved on these signet rings. And so on.

It occurred to Jing, as he heard his brother-in-law speak in English for the first time, that he didn't know the words for pleather or leather. He stared at the belts in his stock and tried to name their colors aloud. Rat, bru, gurene, pingke. Pohpall.

"What?" Hong asked Jing as the potbellied woman moved away.

"Mei you, mei you." Jing waved Hong away, then returned to glowering at his belts. In school, Jing had actually enjoyed English language study, though his low marks suggested otherwise. He was a competent reader, capable of sounding out most words, but he often needed a dictionary to know their meaning.

His pronunciations were terrible. So extraordinarily bad that the English language teacher, a young British woman with cropped red hair even offered to tutor him privately some afternoons. It was she who taught him how to make that fricative sound—the beginning of what seemed to be the most commonly used word in America—thanks. Teacher Inman showed him over and over again. Th, th, th. Her tongue jutted out, curved like a pinkish wave around her teeth.

"Thank you," she said. "No, thank you."

"Theodore Roosevelt." That tongue.

"Thread and needle." Like a pink flower bud.

"Thick and thin." Or a nipple.

. . .

By the end of that month, Jing had not made a single sale. He could contribute nothing to Hong and Mindy's rent and had not replenished any of the hui funds, which he'd spent on the initial expenses of traveling to and setting himself up in New York. As his prospects thinned, the hui's repayment deadline loomed, and it was becoming absurd to think that he could earn enough to repay the neighborhood families before the end of the year.

"I thought it would be easier," he wrote in a letter home, which, for shame, he never sent. He didn't need to consult his mother to know what her response would be. What, in life, had ever made him think that money would come easily?

Hong and Mindy tried to help Jing with his English. They knew how daunting it was. It was difficult enough just to communicate information in foreign words, much less sell or persuade someone to buy something in these words. At the next trade show (at a sand-colored community center in Orange, New Jersey), at Mindy's insistence, Hong pushed his brother-in-law's products whenever he could (though not as hard as he pushed his own). He wrote down a few sentences in English so that Jing could practice conversation starters and product introductions.

"It's just a little crutch, a boost," he said. "What matters is already universal. Everyone can see your products. Everyone can read your prices. It's not a complicated business for us Chinese. Buy, sell, trade from east to west. It's in our history, eh?"

Nights, Mindy instated an English-only kitchen and living room so Jing could practice, but the result was that he simply stopped speaking to them very much.

English: It was full of hard, abrupt endings. No sense of rhythm or lyricism in the words, no awareness of the tonal possibilities. No tones at all. How could it compare to the sonic beauty of their nation's language? How could these twenty-six wormlike shapes compare to the history and artistry of each individual character of the language Han?

"Hell-o. How ah-yoo. How wass yoo day," Jing intoned.

"We are in the presence of a poet and scholar," Hong said.

"Hong. English only," Mindy said.

But Jing could not bear to speak any more of it. "Was this language created by deaf men?"

"It was created by men who wanted to sell as many belts and umbrellas as possible," said Mindy, "to feed their families and pay their debts."

A cool air pushed a few errant maple pods through the open kitchen window. Jing stood to gather them and sweep them out the nearest door. After this, he closed the window, which faced directly into the neighboring kitchen, where he could make out two young girls with heads lowered, working at their books and sheets of paper.

Droplets began to pelt and darken the sidewalk.

"Rain," he said in English.

10

I am dreaming of her when I hear Ellis step gingerly down the stairs. Half-asleep on the couch, I try to place the sounds I hear. The clicking of the gas stove lighting. The bubbling and stuttering of the coffee machine. The tap and scuff of his new slippers. The shush of the chair cushion by the paned glass door that faces our porch.

Eyes closed, I envision the scene—the kitchen, its appliances, Ellis in his tall chair. But I am also remembering, still having, a dream. I saw her face, didn't I? With its dark, absorbing eyes set on high cheeks and those thin, incomplete eyebrows she was always coloring in with a pencil.

"Hey," Ellis says. I jar awake. "You okay? You were breathing really heavily."

It's brighter than my vision of the kitchen was. I squint at the sunlight that cuts into the room.

Ellis touches the side of my face. "And you've got the couch imprinted on you."

Groggy, I sit up to catch my breath and rest my chin on the fleshy bit of Ellis's shoulder. For a while, we sit side by side. Ellis strokes my leg and palms my breasts, which swing loose beneath my unclipped bra. We kiss; he puts a finger in me, but I'm still rattled, distracted by my vision of her. Do I call it a vision, a dream, or a memory? My mother's disembodied head growing larger and larger, floating toward me.

It's not her ghostly face that I can't put out of my mind. The part that frightens me (or that did in the logic of the dream) is that I couldn't read her expression. I couldn't interpret the tilt of her eyebrows, the lines around her mouth, as I had always been able to do before. I realized, with alarm, just before waking: I had never seen this woman before.

*   *   *

For breakfast, I crack three eggs in a bowl, whisk them with a fork. I pour the yellow, globular liquid over an oiled pan on the burner, but it doesn't make a sound. Too early.

I am thinking of my mother by trying not to think about her. I am superstitious enough to know that my dream of her drifting face was a bad omen. I am superstitious enough to believe in omens.

"I think I know what happened, Eleanor," Ellis says.

We're both quiet for a moment, as if we've glitched the system. He looks at me expectantly, and I try to pour a few drops of soy sauce onto the scramble I've made, but too much comes out. Some movement outside the kitchen window catches my attention. Three woolly raccoons pad about the porch, inspecting the scratched wood table and its accompanying moss-covered chairs.

"Just ignore them," Ellis says. "There's nothing edible out there." He pulls two forks from the silverware drawer. It's our routine to eat from a single plate. "I know it was you. The fire. The jerry-rigged heater."

"What are you talking about?" I wave him off, but I can feel myself turning red.

"I went downstairs and saw the thing myself. Next to your mice. You know. The ones that have my name all over them?"

I suppose I knew this was coming. "I know. Okay. I'm sorry." I give a sort of whine. "Did Samir say something? It was an accident. I'll buy a real heater next time."

"Samir? There's no next time, Len. This 'time' is still going on. If they find out it happened under my direction—"

"It wasn't under your direction."

"Exactly," the tines of his fork clink our plate. "The rogue tech who happens to be my wife? That's even worse. You're lucky all we lost were a few papers." One of the raccoons overturns the mostly unused ashtray we keep on a low plastic stool. "It's time to put an end to the side research," Ellis says. He puts a warm palm on my shoulder. "I want to support you. I want the world for you."

"But?"

"But it's all getting out of control," Ellis says. "The hours you spend recording, all the resources. The late nights. It's detracting from your actual job."

"Which is to help you."

"I mean, yes, right. But it isn't just the job. You know that. It's your whole life." He wipes the corner of his mouth with the back of a finger. "Come on. I know it's painful to talk about her. But we have to start somewhere." One of the raccoons picks up the ashtray and sets it back down. It tips and rolls the slope of the short driveway, the glass grinding along the asphalt.

"Eleanor."

"Yes, okay. I'm here. I'm listening. No more projects. I work for you and you alone."

Ellis makes a weak sound of protest. Sunlight glints off the grays at his temples. Outside, the raccoons dawdle, and I fend off an urge to throw something at them. An apple, a wet sponge, a plastic cup. To shoo them off the property with a broom or a shotgun.

11

For a few weeks after the fire, of which everyone learns I am the cause, I give myself over to Ellis. I follow his every move. We share the same schedule again, take the train together to lab and back home again. As he's asked, I give up my unsupervised research projects. It was only a matter of time.

I go to lab, I work. I perform my job dutifully. I spend hours each day performing whatever analysis Ellis needs, minding his mice, etc. I kill mine and end the experiment. I do the work Ellis assigns to me, and I leave it at that. I don't go in at night. I see Samir on occasion, but we are both masterful pretenders and behave as if nothing has changed.

I would describe myself during this time as contented. Ellis and I have sex every few days, or, at least, we give each other hand jobs. We cook together in the evenings. We spend one weekend cleaning out our garage. We spend another weekend in Seattle at a friend's wedding, which renews our own marital devotions all over again. Ellis cooks elaborate, meat-centric meals for dinner. I do his laundry with mine.

I devote myself solely to work and marriage. I sit somewhere outside of myself, which I am very good at doing. "Ellis is the best thing in my life" is my mantra. When he asks around noon if I'm hungry, I always am. When his day at the lab is done, so is mine. For weeks, I am man's best, most loyal friend.

It's not just me. Our lab becomes unusually collaborative and industrious over the course of the weeks that follow the fire. (Really, it wasn't a fire, but the drowned beginnings of one.) The postdocs are even more feverish and self-important. Even Penny, normally reclusive, has taken on a persona I've never seen before. She writes bloc emails updating us on her tireless efforts to secure additional funding to make up for lost time. She asks the postdocs to take over her (paid) teaching responsibilities so that she can focus on these financial and managerial matters. Periodically she emerges from her office to encourage us.

· · ·

Ellis stops eating lunch. He'd been waffling about attending a conference in San Diego, but the fire has renewed his sense of purpose. His eyes dart from one monitor to the other as he makes last-minute touches to his conference poster.

"You go on without me," he says when I stop by his desk one afternoon. "I'll—" he trails, "find the time to eat eventually."

I don't respond when he gets like this about work. Self-sacrificial, over-serious, absent-minded. I go out for lunch. I buy him a burrito.

Two months pass like this. Ellis becomes happier and plumper, like a well-watered plant, and I would be salty about this if the same weren't happening to me. I feel more energetic. I begin even to consider reapplying to the program, picking up where I left off. I've never heard of anyone doing this, but I don't see why I can't be the first. I even return to some of the social events I swore off when I left the program—a birthday happy hour, a talk accompanied by cheap wine and blocks of off-white cheese.

I'd tried to keep up with these events when I first left the program, but it was miserable. I hated the way my friends spoke to me now that I was no longer a part of the cohort, but I felt fragile and ignored when left alone. I felt a sort of indignation that they might combine the fact that my mother was dying, that I'd married Ellis, and that I'd dropped out of the program into one oversimplified conclusion about grief.

I couldn't stand to be reduced, to have conclusions drawn about me. But when no one drew any conclusions, I found myself even more frustrated at the prospect that they weren't thinking about me at all. That they didn't see or care that I was sucking up all the air in the room, replacing it with loss and regret. That we all were. How could they go about chatting and laughing when they could lose someone they loved at any moment? How could anyone keep licking cracker crumbs off their fingers and wiping the wetness from a carrot stick on the pockets of their jeans when they could die later that night for reasons beyond their control?

I was hysterical. But I'm over that now. At happy hour, someone describes me as glowing, and I drink two beers to convince people that I'm not pregnant.

12

But, as I discover several days later, I am.

I guess I was unusually hungover after the beers at happy hour on Thursday, and my stupor didn't dissipate as I moved through the weekend. I was too dizzy that Monday night to offer Ellis a ride to the airport, and the day after he left, my period came. But it was only one day long and petal-pink.

In the women's bathroom on the second floor, I wrap both tests and their cardboard package in the plastic bag they came in. When the bundle is safely unidentifiable, I deposit it in the trash.

Out of habit, I stop into the kitchen to program a coffee before returning to my desk. I am trying to remember the days Ellis and I used protection and the days we didn't, the last night I spent with Samir, the first day of my last period, the period of days during which I might have been ovulating. My mind is swirling with this ovarian calculus, and I'm staring at the wall calendar with such intensity that I don't hear the coffee machine clicking and rasping and spitting up droplets of brown goo.

Samir suddenly appears from the hallway and unplugs the coffee maker. He points to the "out of order" note that has fallen like a weak leaf in front of the microwave.

"First the hair dryer thing, now the coffee machine. You're cursed, woman," Samir says.

My laughter is high and bright in an embarrassing way. I wipe the droplets up with a napkin.

He tilts his head back, as if he needs distance to see all of me. That way he has of looking at me—I feel as if I might cry. For weeks, all interactions between me and Samir have been completely, sociopathically normal. How could two people mimic casual, friendly professionalism so flawlessly? Without having agreed to it beforehand? Lab meetings, happy hours, late evenings preparing for Ellis's last-minute presentation in San Diego. The ease and skill with which we are both able to pretend that there's nothing between us has been so seamless that I've actually started to believe that there's nothing between us.

We decide to go out for coffee, take the elevator, then make our way down Lexington. Samir talks as if we haven't avoided each other's eyes and attentions for the past three weeks. Books he's been reading, gossip he's indulged in. Have I heard about the Harvard student who poisoned her lab's water cooler with sodium azide? Samir heard it from a friend at MIT.

"Did anyone die?"

"No."

"Are they pressing charges?"

"She left with a master's degree."

"They'll just give that shit to anyone, won't they?"

"And then she returned to her home country."

"Where's that?"

Samir slips me a smile. "I don't want to perpetuate any negative stereotypes about your people."

God, I've missed him. But I don't say anything about that.

. . .

Outside, the air is balmy, unseasonably warm. In the bodega, there's an impossible line of customers holding canned beans, dried fruit, boxes of pasta and cereal, jugs of water. The city is preparing for a tropical storm that will touch down tomorrow.

"End of the world as we know it," the man ahead of us says. He holds a single can of cat food. He tips his head at me, and I worry for a moment that he's going to open fire, but he just pays, adjusts his blue paperboy cap, and steps out onto the sidewalk. Only after we order our coffees does the cashier explain to us that the man has already paid for them.

"You wanna pay it forward?" the cashier asks.

I give her a five for the kid behind us.

Samir and I idle in front of the bodega entrance with our coffees. Are his eyes more luminous today beneath the overcast sky? Or have I just forgotten them in the weeks that we've been avoiding each other? I can't remember if pregnant women can drink coffee, so I bring the cup to my lips and mimic swallowing each sip without ingesting anything.

We let faster, busier people navigate their ways around us. Samir leans into me. He brushes his arm to mine, as if by accident, but with Samir there are no accidents. He is both reader and signaler of the faintest, subtlest hints. I must be, too, for how else could we make our way to 96th Street Station without so much as a word about what we are doing and yet doing it anyway?

I start to feel dizzy as we descend underground and sit on an open bench. Samir sits beside me.

"You okay?"

I ought to say something. Something meaningful or clarifying. But I know that breaking the silence will rupture the spell that's binding us together, driving us closer and closer to his apartment.

A train screams forth, bringing with it a wet, musty breeze. A muzzled dog boards the train without an owner in sight, turns around and faces the door.

13

I used to call Samir my brother. I laughed when friends asked if we were secretly sleeping together. My eyes rolled toward the back of my head. Of course not, I said. He's like a brother to me!

We had found each other in the first few weeks of the program when everyone was either openly demanding or quietly construing explanations of one another. What were you researching? How competitive were you academically? How sexually engaged and engaging were you planning to be? Et cetera. Most of us had arrived at Sinai directly after finishing our undergraduate degrees, which meant we had little else but questions of sex and study to categorize each other and understand ourselves by.

But Samir and I seemed to understand each other without much explanation, without the need for polite (though probing) introductory questions. There are some people who just pull every thought out of you, in perfect linear order. Like thick thread through the eye of a needle. What is it that draws you to a stranger? What drew me to Samir?

That year, we took care of each other. We performed little favors for each other. We made each other laugh. The space between us was never charged with competitive or libidinal energy. At least not then. Is this what made me confuse him for a brother? That I couldn't understand or name what it was that electrified the air between us?

We didn't have sex. Not then, anyway. For years, what sustained our friendship, I thought, was that we didn't need to. Once in a blue moon we wound up kissing or entangled on the couch. But somehow, none of it felt quite real or erotic. Yes, there were nights that my hand traveled up and down the length of Samir's leg, but I could never will it to arrive at any particular destination. Doing so would have broken something else we shared, something fragile and worth keeping.

After I met Ellis, the tension between me and Samir sort of dissipated. In some ways it was a relief. Things with Samir had become impossible to interpret. Meanwhile, Ellis was direct, guileless. What he wanted from me (at least early on) was unequivocal, and I could respond with a simple yes or no. Dating, or not dating. Sex, or no sex. Things could be simple if I only allowed them to be.

. . .

Samir's apartment is stifling. Beside the bed is a reading chair, which functions as a shelf for textbooks and a few paperbacks. There's a trio of mini cacti on the windowsill.

The mattress is on the floor, wrapped like a gift—the thin, pilled blanket tucked between the bed and the floor. A framed poster of Radiohead's *Kid A* hangs on the wall, and two perfectly even stacks of textbooks serve as a table at the foot of the bed.

I remain where I am on top of the covers, which are damp from his back, then mine, then his again. It's extremely hot, and I reach to open a window.

Samir leaves the room and returns holding a tall glass bottle of water by the neck. A thick breeze blows through the open window as he fills two of the many empty glasses that are sitting on the windowsill.

Is it the heat or the sex? I feel like a blunted tool. For a minute, I watch the bottle sweat by the window and search for what to say. I ask how his girlfriend is doing, but he doesn't really take the bait.

"She's good. Same old."

Samir's eyes flit across my face, but he doesn't say anything more.

"This is probably the last time we can do this," I say into my glass. The water is so cold it stings my teeth.

"Do what?" Samir plays.

"I can't be two people, right? I have to make a decision."

"That's a loaded question. A neuroscientist is probably the wrong person to ask."

I'm acutely aware of the desire rising in me to tell him that I'm pregnant. But I know that it will sever things between us, no matter who I think the father is. And anyway, I haven't finished my menstrual calculations yet. Does it matter to me who the father is? Or is it something that would only matter to them?

In the perfect stillness of Samir's bedroom, I try to think of what my mother would tell me to do in that imperious tone of hers. But it's impossible to conjure her. Why? Why is she hiding herself from me? I experience a brief, irrational flash of anger and then I immediately put it aside.

I explain to Samir that things with Ellis are going pretty well. "That's why I've been kind of MIA." My throat twitches. "I think maybe this is a goodbye."

Samir nods, pushes his hair against its current grain. "Again?" He fishes for his shirt under the pillow beside me. "You don't have to explain yourself to me," he says when he sees my expression. "We love each other, right? Part of that is just that we watch out for each other. Ellis is a good guy. Accomplished, stable, not a narcissist. He took care of you when your mom passed away. I want all that for you. I'm happy for you. Honestly."

"But what do you want for you?" I ask.

"Ugh," he waves my question away, slips into a pair of ill-fitting jeans. "Do we have to do this? If you're happy, I'm happy. So are you happy?"

The question feels like a trap; I don't answer.

Samir lowers himself to the floor, collects a black hair tie from underneath a wooden stool, then hands it to me. "Just," he says, "don't make me this person."

"What person?" I rough my shirt over my head and tie my hair in a knot.

"The object of your manipulations. You know, where you try to suss out what the other person is *feeling*—" he says the word with some repugnance—"so you can adjust your own behavior accordingly? Don't laugh. I know you, Eleanor. I know all about it. Maybe I do the same thing. Maybe it's what makes us get along so well. But I prefer not to be manipulated. If you're happy, then so am I. If you're not, then do whatever you need to do. I would never hold that against you."

A pigeon purrs somewhere outside the open, grated window.

"That's not what you wanted to hear, I guess," he adds carefully.

"I just don't think I even fully understand what you're saying."

"I'm saying: Don't talk me into wanting something I can't have."

I make a big show of looking for my phone, and after we find it on the kitchen counter, I collect my purse and show myself out.

14

I lied about never having been pregnant before. Once, I was.

It came from a disagreement. We were drunk from the wine we'd had at his parents' house, where Ellis announced clumsily before dinner had even started that we would be getting married.

"Oh?" his mother, Lydia, called from the kitchen, in a voice meant for children who don't know they're misbehaving.

"Well, yes. We're in love," Ellis said plainly, which I found embarrassingly naive.

"Wonderful," his father said. "And her parents? Did you ask for their blessing? Or did you proclaim it like this?"

"It's just her mom," Ellis said.

"Oh," Lydia lilted sorrowfully. Then, catching herself, added a bright, "Okay!"

"But we have her blessing," I said, ambitious for theirs. "She loves Ellis. She's thrilled that we met." Could they see that I was lying? "She calls it destiny that I went to Mount Sinai and met Ellis there. In Chinese, it's called yuan fen," I overenunciated. "Yuan fen. Fate, basically."

There were hugs and kisses after that. Ellis's dad opened a bottle of red but insisted that it tasted of vinegar and had to be dumped out. He rummaged in the cabinet and found a white instead.

When I think of it now, I guess I hadn't seriously thought we were getting married. Just like I hadn't seriously understood that I could get pregnant. I have a problem of directly, even boldly, courting ideas that seem utterly and impossibly abstract. Getting married was on par with other fantasies Ellis and I had entertained—living abroad, starting a privately funded lab, learning to scuba dive, learning Portuguese. Sure, it was within the realm of possibility, but it wasn't actually going to happen to us, was it? I had stupidly failed to notice that in my total disbelief of its likelihood, I was the one welcoming the idea, nudging us into the orbit of marrying.

Once we'd announced the idea to Ellis's parents, I understood my mistake immediately. Marriage would be the end of me. It was the end of every woman.

When I said as much to Ellis, he listened with patience and some amusement. I could tell from the softness of his brow that he didn't take my worries seriously, that he thought I was being skittish and dramatic. Maybe I was. He tugged at the lobe of my ear, pushed a mess of hair away from my cheek. "That's just what love feels like," he said. "I feel it, too." He wedged his leg between the two of mine. "That's how I know we were made for each other," he said.

But we were not made for each other. He had not been made for anyone. Only I, beaten sex that I was, had been made for him. Love would not change this (though I did love him and believe I still do). Love had nothing to do with it.

Still, I found myself swayed by his reassurances, grateful for them. I kissed his ear and his lips. I clung to him, rode him, let my hair fall like a curtain around his face. I gripped his shoulders. I was desperate. I pushed myself onto him. I felt as though I were eating him, swallowing him whole, and when I lifted myself off of him, I knew I would be pregnant.

.   .   .

Our girl grew. In those first months, we would never have described her as an accident. We called her our passion. We called her our dream. Our best and all-time favorite secret. We told no one and reveled in the secrecy. At home, we were dizzied and excited to be parents. We examined my body for signs and symbols; we researched names for their sounds and then for their etymologies. We careened from name to name, Greek origins, Latin roots, Chinese homages. Ellis liked the sound of French names, though I thought in American English they sounded a bit ridiculous.

"You can hardly pronounce them," I said, laughing, and we spent a few minutes intoning French names until my mother called.

"What's wrong? Are you drunk?" she asked when she heard me stifling my laughter.

In the outside world, at the lab, among friends and family, we did our best to remain inconspicuous. We hardly made eye contact when we saw each other; like secret lovers. I didn't have a very obvious pregnancy, and this pleased us. Every day we (a family!) commuted to the lab, worked a full day, returned home, and no one seemed to notice a thing.

Penny wrote to me once to ask if we were doing okay, why Ellis and I were avoiding each other. Aside from this, no one batted an eye, cast a single glance. That we shared her with no one but each other was an integral part of our joy. She was ours and no one else's.

There is often no way of knowing what causes miscarriages to occur. "It could have been anything" seems to be a common phrasing in the obstetric community. It could also have been nothing. That collective physician's shrug.

"She's a sanctimonious dud," I said from the passenger's seat of the car. "Why doesn't she just say what she means? 'We don't care enough to know. Sincerely, we do not want to know. Our jobs would be harder. Life would be worse if we knew how to prevent all your pathetic, failed attempts at giving birth.'"

More hatred for my obstetrician frothed from within me. I cursed her knitted eyebrows, the warm hand she had placed briefly on my shoulder.

"Stop, please," Ellis said.

"Even auto mechanics know more about their trade."

"Len."

"We know more about the birth of the fucking sun," I said, "than we do about—"

I knew I was wrong, spouting pure, bilious nonsense. But I had supped from what seemed to be an inexhaustible spring of self-pity. I waited for a comforting word, but Ellis said nothing. The profile of his face was sunken and gray. I turned away from him. In the window's reflection, I looked tired, too.

Our story changed. Really, she had been an accident, a product of impulse. We began understanding her as such. We began understanding her not as a "her" at all. Of course, she would have made us happy. She would have changed us forever. But so would many things in our long life together, Ellis consoled.

"Some days," I would corroborate, "I didn't really want her."

A Good Woman
Changes Everything

"Ah-tumn," Jing murmured to himself. "Faw." He was embarrassed to say the words. You had to make your mouth so tall to say them. It was undignified.

That fall, the pin oak leaves turned a bright and unnerving shade of red. The air became dry and thin. In the cold, it was difficult to inhale. Or was it too easy? Perhaps he wasn't accustomed to so much oxygen? It was hard to tell. Jing was the sort of man who could not diagnose a problem, though he knew it was there.

Jing could sense his sister and her husband distancing themselves from him, preparing to lop him off the body of their two-headed household. Who could blame them? He was able to contribute less and less to the monthly rent, to the costs of utilities and groceries. The sample stock collected dust in the closet as Jing's resolve for entrepreneurial success began to wane. He didn't have the stamina.

He took up a cleaning job at a local gym. How strange and intimate it was to see these men and women exercising. Especially the women. These women and their bright, clingy clothes. What were they doing? Stepping up on a plastic platform and stepping back down, shouting and whooping, sashaying side to side, as if their whole mission were to bounce their parts back and forth, up and down. It was mesmerizing and obscene.

Needless to say, some women complained to management about the skinny Asian cleaner who stared. One woman even cursed directly at him while he was distractedly mopping the hallway near the open-plan aerobics room.

"The hell are you looking at?" she'd said, hands on square hips.

The small wires of hair by her forehead were matted with sweat, and a pink glow haloed her cheeks and forehead. Farther down, a wide darkened triangle revealed the outline of her sweat-saturated panties beneath her shorts. Jing looked away, pushed the mop back and forth on the wood-paneled floors.

"That's what I thought," the woman said. She turned to face the instructor at the front of the room, but this only revealed to Jing another triangle of dampness. He kept at his work. There was such a thing as too much freedom.

Jing was transferred to the night shift. Fine with him. He was grateful for the evenings away from his sister and brother-in-law, who seemed now to vibrate with disapproval of him. Of course, Jing had known that their hospitality, almost ostentatious at first, would close in on itself like a fist. What he had not accounted for was his continued dependency on them.

Jing slept fitfully in the daytime, on his sister's couch. Sometimes he partook in lustful thoughts about that dark, wet woman with the square hips and broad chest. Other times it was a young Doris Day who colonized the sleeper's mind. He tried not to worry over the letters from his mother, which accumulated in a metal tin beneath the couch. But against his will, his brain had memorized their contents already.

In the tin, Jing also stored a roll of bills. The amount seemed always to hover just under forty dollars, and he begrudged the idea of parting with his only possession (or means to possess) in order to chip away at a debt that was one hundred times as much.

He drank beers, he dabbled in cards with Hong and his friends. He luxuriated in the warm, brightly lit laundromats rather than washing and scrubbing his clothes in the tub. That is to say, he spent what he earned on himself. He was a bad son.

While Jing worked at night, Mindy rummaged through his belongings. She counted the cash and read the letters from their mother. It was from these letters that she learned the gossip of the neighborhood. Weiping had attempted suicide, Ailian had eloped with a Taiwanese local to Kenting to live on the beach. Their younger brother, Ah Mao, was up to something shady, but she couldn't quite tell what it was. Did Jing have any ideas? (Of course, he wouldn't, Mindy thought. Jing had lived his twenty years in Taiwan as if he'd known all along he would spirit away from it one day. He'd likely forgotten Weiping and Ailian and all the dramas of life in Taipei.)

From the latest letter, Mindy also learned that their mother believed Jing was attending university. That any day now he might receive a scholarship, the bulk of which he could send back to pay the members of this maternal hui.

When will the money be repaid? The ladies have stopped inviting me to gatherings. They are plotting against me, probably. Where is the money, my eldest son? Do you expect me to die of shame? I am avoided and whispered about. Send word, or they will all think you've stolen away with our money. Jing, how is school? Did the university grant any scholarship? I know it's hard to study in America, but don't forget it's hard to stay behind, too.

Mindy capped the tin and returned it to the exact position and location where she had found it. So her brother was a liar and a thief. Had he planned to run away with the neighborhood's money, leaving their mother to contend with the wrath of a group of jilted amateur lenders? She had defended Jing so many times from her husband, who was closer each day to evicting her naive and unambitious brother.

Mindy had counseled patience. "He has no place to go. Either here with us or back to Taiwan."

Hong: "Should I feel sorry for him? I'd punt him back myself if I could."

. . .

In November, there was a new letter in the box, recently added to the top of the stack of a mother's concern, rage, and defeat. Mindy lifted the letter from the tin. She swore it smelled of jasmine and fragrant white rose, but perhaps she was homesick.

Esteemed Jing,

It's been six months since you left for New York. Are you well?

Let's be dry and crisp about this: I am not angry you didn't marry me. I have no feelings about it whatsoever. Don't ask a question if you can only handle one answer. Remember Teacher Yu would say that? Very wise.

I wanted to give you some updates. The entire neighborhood is waiting for you to send the money back, which you owe. Zhang Wei is saving money to go to graduate school at Tatung University, and if she doesn't have enough, she can't go. Ah Di broke his leg like a fool while riding his motorcycle in a typhoon. (Everyone knows it's his own fault. He rode all the way to Banqiao to meet a girl in a rainstorm.) I'm reminding you in case you forgot: Life goes on here even after you've left. We still need what we needed before. (I am talking about the money.)

I took the liberty of translating this letter into English for you on the next page. Not that you'll understand it. Everyone knows the Liu family brothers have terrible English. Everyone except the Liu brothers. (Ha ha I'm just kidding.) Maybe your English has improved, but I suspect it hasn't. I know you better than you think, brother. For instance, I know you would never be frivolous with money. You are a good and cautious man, Jing. A bit of a bunny, in fact. Which means you aren't sending money home because you don't have any.

Thus, I believe it is in your best interest to hire me. I have a mind for money and accounting, as you remember. My English is excellent, as I've proven. More than we can say for you.

I have the money to get myself to New York. I can take care of myself. What I need is a piece of paper with a man's name on it, inviting me.

Please respond.

Your good friend,
Li Huiwen

Mindy thrust the letter to Hong, who shook his head. "I don't want to read his letters."

"It's Huiwen." She dodged the arm Hong held out against her, a frail attempt to block his wife from involving him in her problems. "She needs papers to immigrate."

"What do I care about what she needs?"

"She was a fine girl, wasn't she? She and Jing would be all right."

"I see why your brother is the way he is. He has two mothers. Now you want to find him a third."

Mindy ignored him. She brought out a pen and a sheet of the thick paper Hong reserved for his showy letters home. She wrote to Huiwen in Jing's terse voice, that formal way of writing and speaking he had. Never relaxed or at ease. Always at risk of saying some wrong and irrevocable thing.

Hong stood by as Mindy penned a letter to Huiwen. He kicked at the mass of belongings that Jing pushed into the corner each afternoon before he left for the gym. Shoes and inserts that softened the nightly wear on his soles. Languishing English textbooks, dog-eared pamphlets collected from subway solicitors and crazy people. Clothes, hung on the back and arms of the chair Hong used to sit in, to clip his anemic nails, read the paper.

When she was done, Mindy glued the flap of the envelope down and tucked it into her purse to be posted the next morning. Then, she removed a half pound of flank from the refrigerator and began her cut across the grain.

. . .

Four months later, Rita arrived in New York. How to explain her first step onto US soil: Have you ever seen a woman with stars in her eyes? The airy halls of LaGuardia Airport were decorated with red and green trimmings, gargantuan teddy bears and snow creatures, striped candies, gold stars and silver bells.

Men and women sped by—no rhyme or reason (that Rita could discern) to their facial features or their ways of dress. Some families and couples wore floral dresses, diaphanous scarves, floral leis around their pig-pink necks. Others wore long, boxy coats, luxurious, fur-trimmed hats and gloves. People clopped along in spurred western-style boots, wrapped their heads in scarves of brilliant blues, purples, reds. She saw heads of hair streaked with pink and green. She met eyes underlined with thick black and shaded over with brilliant blue. A group of broad-shouldered girls in matching red sweat suits bowled past her, shouting and guffawing as they went.

"That's America," Jing said when Rita remarked on the sheer variety of dress and appearance she had encountered. "They like to dress themselves up to be different from everyone else. Individualism." He said it as if diagnosing an incurable illness.

"Ai, nonsense," Mindy said in that didactic tone the elder sibling adopts. "We're at an American airport. It's the most varied and diverse place in all the world."

She shepherded Rita and Jing toward the line for yellow taxis. Jing tried to take Rita's suitcase, but she scowled at him, yanked the leather handle out of his reach. This country bumpkin, he thought.

There was the immediate and familiar stench of cigarette smoke and, puzzlingly, of urine, and both took on a sharper, more acidic pungency in the bitter cold. The air was crisp, which made it almost painful to breathe. The sky was starless but vibrant with red and yellow lamps and bulbs. The driver stood by as Rita loaded her bags into the trunk. No one spoke as the cab lurched toward Elmhurst.

That week, Rita and Mindy slept in the bedroom together underneath separate quilts while Hong slept on the pullout couch in the living room. Jing was demoted to a sturdy metal cot purchased at the military surplus store.

Rita had guessed that Jing's business was flopping, but she could not have guessed that he had given up so entirely. His face was puffy and sallow from lack of sleep. She knew that he worked as a cleaner late into the night, but was that his only source of income? His belly protruded over the once-black pants of his janitorial uniform.

"Didn't you say that business was going well?" Rita asked one afternoon while both Mindy and Hong were at work.

It was just after noon, and she had listened to him return home at five in the morning. The unzipping and folding of his pants, the shallow sigh before wrestling with the papery bedding wrapped around the cot. Later in the morning, she dressed and folded the sheets and blankets, laid them neatly on Mindy's bed. She moved gingerly around Jing for a few hours, cooking breakfast, tidying her own things, cooking lunch.

And at noon, she decided it was time to wake her employer up. He'd brought her here, hadn't he? What was his plan? She kicked the peg of the cot where Jing was sleeping. "Where's this warehouse you were looking for?"

"Eh?"

"In the letter. You said you were going to rent a warehouse where all your inventory would go. Where we could work together. That's why I sent you the money."

"The chives are burning," Jing said.

Rita rushed back to the stovetop, moved the pan away from the fire.

Jing stretched his legs. "My sister wrote the letter. She didn't tell you yet?"

Rita felt the hairs prick up and away from the skin of her neck. "To fleece me?"

"You got what you wanted, didn't you? Your papers?"

Rita clattered the pan into the sink and ran water over the black bits. What she had wanted was Jing—plain and simple. But the plainer and simpler her desire, the more she felt that she must protect it from the light of day. Move toward it in circuitous paths, at odd, oblique angles.

What was it about Jing Liu? Why did she trust him? It was something she would ask herself all her life. What was it in him that was so special to her that she felt, more than anything, a need to shelter and protect? He had a special power over her that she could not name or even describe. But why? He could hardly be called charming. They had never kissed or even touched.

"Ai, Huiwen," her mother had bemoaned while Rita packed her bag. "They all have something special about them. They all cast some sort of spell. But, a woman shouldn't travel so far for a man. If he really wants you, he should come back to fetch you."

"I'm going for a job." Rita snatched the letter back from her mother's hand, but this was deeply unconvincing.

Her mother sighed. "My daughter is daft, and I never knew until today."

Now Rita laid out a few unappealing dishes for lunch. "Is there even a business to work for?" she asked.

"Sure." Jing stood and motioned at the closet, where the boxes of his original samples were shoved into its deep recesses. On top of them lay a crumpled order of women's socks that had been returned for its embarrassing lack of quality control. "You can have it. Consider my thief sister's debt repaid."

. . .

Rita and Jing were married early the next year in an intimate ceremony with Mindy and Hong serving as witnesses. The truth was that Rita did not much care whether Jing's business was flourishing or failing. His failure to secure a foothold in the US somehow only entrenched her love for him more deeply. She was bolstered by the fact that she still wanted him in spite of his failings. It felt pure, loving someone this way. Was there anything more freeing than wanting someone so fearlessly? Without qualm, or caution, or reservation. As only a man or a child could love.

"Yuan fen," Mindy said over their celebratory dinner at Golden Unicorn, tears budding at the inner corners of her eyes. "These two. Friends since childhood and now partners in life and marriage."

"What yuan fen?" Hong said. "It was all thanks to your meddling."

"Yes, I'm grateful to Da jie, our cupid." Rita supped at her tea, let the jasmine steam rise and warm her nose.

Jing gave them all a smile and ate disinterestedly. Had he come all the way to America, stolen from his own mother, so that he could marry Rita, a girl he'd known all his life? A Chinese bumpkin just like him? From the same city, the same schools, the same neighborhood? In truth, he would never forgive his sister for selling him to Rita in this way. He moved a piece of short rib about his mouth, letting it rest at different angles on different molars. Each tooth played its part in gnawing meat off the bone.

"Jing understands now." Rita poured everyone's tea deftly, without looking. "A good woman changes everything."

. . .

It turned out that Rita was as useful as she had claimed to be (if not more). What a saleswoman she was. What a charmer. She had a lovely, chiming laugh. She flirted. Most impressive was the remarkable ability Rita had for learning new words in English, and for modulating the way those words sounded. She could turn her accent up and down, as if it were controlled by a smooth, dark knob.

Demand for Jing's wares picked up within weeks of Rita's arrival. Of course, a woman was needed to sell wigs and hair accessories and shoelaces and belts. These were women's things, after all. At trade shows in New York, Connecticut, Baltimore, Rita closed wholesale orders mainly on belts (it helped that she wore them around her svelte waist) and costume wigs.

Within a year, they'd expanded quickly to other products. What an appetite Americans had for cheap toys, little gifts and temporary nonsense. And how easy it was for Chinese people to satiate this hunger. Neither maker nor buyer seemed to care that these items were shoddily constructed. That was part of the luxury. To hold an ephemeral object, something whose life began to wane the moment you started to use it. Something that told you you would outlast it, it would not outlast you.

. ♦ .

Orders for toys and children's things grew larger and more frequent. They rented a modest warehouse (as Mindy had envisioned!) in New Jersey where they could store their items and begin assembling more complicated products—like the hair accessories that their daughters would come to know the warehouse for.

Three years passed this way—with Rita at the helm of Jing's ship. It was a period of great prosperity for the two of them. They sent money to their mothers, repaid the hui. They repaid Jing's debt to his sister (which, unbeknownst to Jing, Mindy had been tabulating for all those months in a small, spiral notepad).

Rita and Jing worked well together. Their partnership thrived. Rita chatted in her easy English with buyers at trade shows and whipped through the account books in the warehouse office. Jing managed the warehouse, hiring workers and showing them what to assemble and how. Every few months, his brother Ah Mao sent boxes filled with assorted products from sellers in Taiwan.

Jing was not a very good salesperson, but he was an astute, discerning buyer. "Good enough" was Jing's buying mantra, and it served him well. He pulled at the ribbons and weaves to see when loose threads would appear. He clipped and unclipped pins and fasteners to see how much activity they could withstand. He ran everything under a stream of water in the sink. Did the dyes run? Did the glue dissolve? He looked for evidence of immediate wear. The early inklings of disintegration.

For months, they lived in the warehouse's poorly ventilated second floor. They laid mats and blankets down and slept together on the floor among shipments of dollar store items—bangles, hair bands, nail kits, plastic children's gifts and toys stocked by mini-golf courses, movie theaters, theme parks.

Soon after that, Rita got a contract with a chain of video arcades in the tristate area. They left the warehouse for a clapboard house that sat on a canal. They were happy to look out onto any body of water, even if it was rumored to carry trace amounts of radiation from the nuclear power plant upstream. From their bedroom window, Rita had a view of the dark water reflecting a bright, birdless sky.

15

The storm comes and goes without calamitous effect. There's little loss of power, and certainly no shortage of dried goods or potable water. NJ Transit has its usual share of morning commuters. Do they look vaguely disappointed to be on their way to work, or is it just that I am vaguely disappointed to be on my way to work? Vibrant, green leaves litter the sidewalks and streets, giving the city a festive look.

On campus, workers and contractors are collapsing orange vinyl tubes and removing sand-filled barriers from the entrances of buildings. I spend the morning with the other techs and some grad students reversing all the interim flood-prevention measures that were put into place (by us) the previous night.

There are animals everywhere. We evacuated them from the basement floors as a precaution against drowning, and now caged lab mice, cats, songbirds, marmosets are dispersed everywhere, on every floor in almost every lab. We ferry them back to their habitats in the lower levels, which feel cool and somewhat damp but are otherwise unaffected.

After the animals are carted home, I look into the cages of Ellis's mice, which I stacked on his desk last night. For animals who have just spent their first night outside of a light- and temperature-controlled room, they seem unimpressed. They huddle in a corner, and one of them nibbles at a toy. I message Ellis and ask how the conference is going, but it's early on the West Coast, and he doesn't answer.

Once his mice are fed, cage-cleaned, and accounted for, I return to my desk and focus. I try to detect bloating or nausea, any gastrointestinal sensation at all. All morning I have been hyperaware of my body and any symptoms of pregnancy it might reveal to me. Am I nauseous or hungry? I eat two blueberry muffins leftover from a talk from this morning. Am I nauseous now or just overfull? They say that those who can't properly handle excitement experience it as anxiety. I make myself a cup of tea. When it's cold, I pour it out in the kitchen sink.

Samir is nowhere to be found. Not that I'm actively looking for him. I see no sign of him as I pass by his desk to make another cup of tea, and pass by again to wash my mug, and pass by again on my way to Penny's office. No sweatshirt hanging from the back of his chair. Black monitor. But I am not looking for him, and therefore his absence has no impact on me. A stir bar clinks endlessly in a glass flask on his desk. I resist the urge to text him.

. . .

I am standing in the elevator bank when Tingwei calls from behind me. She moves crazily, looking at me and then past me, up at the ceiling and in every doorway she passes. Strands of her wiry hair lie flat against her forehead.

I ask her if she's okay.

"You were here last night, weren't you?" She smells of stale coffee.

"Yeah, you saw me."

"You helped move the animals upstairs? What did you move exactly?"

I quickly recount everything I'd had a part in. I'd stacked other researchers' mice on top of Ellis's and carried them up to their respective labs. I'd cooed at the marmosets and played bright videos on my phone for them while Tingwei herself (the colony manager) and some other researchers sedated them. After the marmosets, I'd helped move some songbirds into an open hallway.

"Well, we're missing one," Tingwei says, stopping me. "A marmoset. We should have twenty-three. We only have twenty-two." She looks down at her tablet, as if to confirm that the numbers remain the same.

I didn't see anything unusual, I tell her, but really, I'd spent most of the evening moving the mice, of which there are hundreds. "Have you tried security? They might even have some video you can look through."

"I haven't reported him missing yet. I don't want to get anyone fired." She looks down at her tablet again. "You know what I mean?"

"I'll keep it to myself. I won't say anything to anyone. Whose animal is it? They might've thought we would be out for a few days and taken him home. It's happened before," I say, trying to sound reassuring. "Maybe wait another day before you report it."

She nods, but she isn't listening. "Sig is so adventurous, too. So maybe he's just around."

"Sig?"

"Short for Sigmund."

Oh, God. I let slip a roll of the eyes. These primate people. They tell us not to anthropomorphize, not to see ourselves everywhere we look. But then they go and name their animals after us, after everyone we know.

"And the sedatives make him so loopy," she frets. I put a reassuring hand on her shoulder. We're quiet for a moment as if mourning a lost friend.

"So are you saying you think Sig is loose in the building?"

She sighs. "I'm saying it would be the best-case scenario if he were still in the building." She thanks me for keeping it quiet for now, then spots someone else to question and flies down the hall.

On my way back to my desk, I catch a wave of slick black hair and dark, triangular eyebrows over one of the desk separators. My stomach turns with nerves. I move toward him, but it turns out to be a different grad student with his hair smoothed back.

Hello, I text him.

I sort of fucked up, I write.

Where are you? Could use some help.

And later: Are you ignoring me?

16

At home, it smells strongly of piss. The apples I cut up are wet, browned, and scattered across the floor. The sugared peanuts are gone. The ceramic bowl that housed them sits upside down on a copy of *Moby-Dick*, which has retained its position perfectly centered on the coffee table. (It's Ellis's. He's been working at it for years. Whenever he feels like he's forgotten the thread of things, he starts over.)

The kitchen smells of feces, but I can't determine its source from where I stand. A glass vase I haven't seen in a while lies precariously on one of the padded chairs by the kitchen table. Inside it sits the tennis ball I left for Sig to play with.

I hear a chirp from the living room, where Sig is rubbing his chest and genitals on the corner of the couch. He turns to look at me as I lock the door behind me and slip off my shoes.

"Hi," I say cheerily.

He starts to howl.

Christ. I never think before I act. And frankly the thinking after the acting produces few results. But you have to understand that Sig attached himself to *me* last night.

The marmosets normally inhabit a large, white-walled, L-shaped habitat on the bottommost floor of the building. This was one of the major flood risks last night, and we spent hours sedating the marmosets and then depositing their limp bodies in carry boxes, which we carted up to the third floor. There, each animal would be held in its own cage until the storm passed.

After an hour or so in the marmoset habitat, it became overcrowded with frantic grad students, stressed marmosets, and a very flustered Tingwei. Dayo, one of the grad students, and I decided to split up our tasks. She ferried the cart of marmosets upstairs, and I placed the sedated animals into individual cages. That way Dayo could return the cart and carry-boxes downstairs while I remained to record each animal's name, heart rate, etc.

Storm winds lashed at the building. "This is crazy." Dayo looked out the window as she pushed the empty cart toward the door. "They better reimburse our cab rides, right?"

She left, but I didn't want her to. It made me sad to review what we'd done, to see the rows of small, limp bodies. Initially, I was sort of happy when Sig woke up. He chirped and whimpered, faint in comparison to the wind. I threw him a marshmallow from one of the bins, but he batted it away. It landed on the floor of the cage below him, next to a marmoset that didn't move.

Sig shook and howled at the cage's wired walls. I tried my best to stay calm, but "loopy" cannot even begin to describe his wild, febrile panic. Somehow, he shook the cage door loose and leapt out at my chest, grabbing the lapel of my jacket. I admit I shrieked. I tried to uncurl his fingers from their grip on my jacket and deposit him in the empty cage. He let go but seized my hair. My offers of nuts and raisins only wound up on the ground.

Eventually, I calmed down, which calmed Sig down. Once I stood still, Sig's grip loosened. He began to move, burrowing into my coat pocket, or the crook of my arm. I sat down at an unused desk and let him familiarize himself with my body. I sat for so long that the room's motion-sensitive lights went out. Raindrops glittered on the windows. In the black computer screen in front of me, I could make out a reflection of my own face: tired. Every part of it trending downward.

Sig tilted his head every which way with a sort of birdlike spasticity. Maybe the darkness calmed him. Don't anthropomorphize, they say. But what else do we have to understand the world by?

I tried handing him another marshmallow. I watched in the dark reflection as he took it from my hand and nibbled. He clambered up to my shoulder, and I fed him there. He curled around my neck, and I fed him there. I parted the slim interior pocket of my coat and dropped a handful of treats inside, and in Sig climbed. Tiny palms prodded at my ribs, my belly, the side of my breast. I felt him make my body his home.

17

Sig is still screeching as I clear all the books and travel souvenirs from the narrow bookshelf by the television. I shouldn't have left him here, even for a few hours, but I felt I had to show my face at the lab. I pour some raisins from a red box onto one of the emptied shelves, and Sig climbs dutifully toward it, nibbles while I clean the rest of the house. Whenever I pause to check on him, I find him staring at me. I mop up the piss from the floors.

I collect a few small tubers of fecal matter and put them together in one corner of the living room on a piece of cardboard, which I secure to the floor with duct tape. I lay a flat sheet over the blue chair by the window, which is stained with urine, and which Sig immediately scent-marks again before returning to his perch on the highest shelf. Briefly, I consider scent-marking the house with my own urine.

. . .

When Samir knocks at the door, I instinctively shush Sig, who is chattering with himself, playing with the tennis ball I've cut into quarters for him to piece back together. He moves toward me, plucks at my socks, and climbs up my leg to check the pocket of my jeans.

"What the hell is this," Samir says when he sees us from the doorway.

"Can you close the door? Like right now." I hustle Samir inside. His eyes widen as he takes stock of the room around him. He presses his lips together, and when he releases them, I can see the blood rush back into them. "Everyone," he says, "is looking for that marmoset."

"Yes, I know." I lean against the countertop. I tell him everything about last night. How frightened Sig was by the storm winds, by all the limp bodies of his family and friends in those cages. How I hadn't had the heart to leave him there. That he'd clung to me for dear life.

Samir looks at me as if I'm unhinged. "Tingwei is ripping her hair out looking for him."

"I know, I know." I shake my head as if I'm standing in disapprobation of someone else. Some other Eleanor whose behavior I don't endorse or even understand. But I'm very aware of having to suppress a smile. Something in me feels gleeful at the prospect of a secret between us.

"What's the goal here, exactly? What are you trying to do?" Sig pulls at the tongue of Samir's sneaker. "Please don't tell me this is a save-the-animals thing?"

What am I trying to do here? It's a question with no answer. Why is it so easy to anthropomorphize Sig and yet so difficult to anthropomorphize myself? Why is it always as if I'm feeling my way out of a dark room?

"It was kind of an accident." I shrug.

"This is a crazy thing to call an accident."

Sig climbs up the leg of Samir's pants and reaches into the pocket of his coat. Finding nothing, he hops to the counter, then leaps to the high, conquering shelf.

I want badly to touch him, but when I try to wrap my arms around him, Samir stands stiff, and when I let go, he moves across the room. He sits in the sagging blue wing chair, and I don't have the heart to tell him it's been pissed on by a monkey.

"Bring him back tonight. I'll help you."

"I think I don't want to."

"I'm very confident that Sinai will press charges."

"Not if they don't know I'm involved."

"But now I'm also involved."

"I suppose you shouldn't say anything about it then."

We volley fruitlessly like this for a minute more.

"Tingwei will never forgive you." Samir searches me for a weak spot. "You can forget being accepted back into the program. You'll lose your job. You'll embarrass Ellis."

I put up a hand. "Stop. Stop the caring and the advising."

A dimple appears on Samir's face. "You texted *me*," he says. He stands and offers a palm to Sig who touches the outstretched fingers, turns the hand over to inspect the other side.

"Just drop the caretaking-older-brother act."

Samir tilts his head at Sig but leaves his hand where it is. "It's not an act. I care about you."

"Why? What's the end goal of caring about me?"

Samir's brow lifts up toward his hairline. "The end goal . . ."

This is all very embarrassing. I should retreat. But the words just sort of gurgle out. "We always pretend it's all about me. About taking care of me, my grief, my problems, my marriage. But what do *you* want? Do you want me? Do you want to leave your girlfriend?" I can't even say her name. "Do you want me to leave Ellis?"

A very loud knocking at the front door startles us both and sends Sig into a frenzy. From the curtainless bay window, I can see my neighbor standing at a distance from the door, holding his cell phone up like a holy cross.

"I knew it," he announces when I open the door to him. He lunges in, panning our open floor plan with his phone. "That thing"—he motions to Sig with a jerk of the head— "was screaming all day. My dogs didn't know what the hell was going on. Some kind of chimp. You can't have that thing here. Absolutely no way you can have that here."

"Harris, okay." I try to speak over him, but he keeps repeating himself as he records me, Samir, Sig, our surroundings.

"No way that's allowed. No way in hell." He derives energy from his own outrage. The more he tells me that exotic animals are not permitted according to the neighborhood rules, the more exact language he seems to remember from the bylaws. He fuels himself. A kind of frantic, law-enforcing ouroboros. "No reptiles, no lions, no tigers, no apes, no potentially dangerous creatures. Not permitted under any circumstances."

"Okay, sir? We're getting rid of it, but you need to calm down," Samir says, stepping out onto the front stoop.

"*Me* calm down?" Harris's eyes bulge at me as if to ask why this stranger is addressing him. "You're lucky you don't see Animal Control parked on the curb after all I've seen today."

"Harris." I turn toward him. "You really can't be looking into our windows when we aren't home."

Our neighbor ignores me, pushes his chest forward. "Who is this guy? Where's your husband at? I want to talk to him."

I start to inform Harris that I'll pass the message along, but before I can, he lets out a sort of yelp and points behind me.

Sig leaps from the tall shelf to the space above the kitchen cabinets where we keep old bottles and vases and other objects we don't need. He leers at us with bright, attentive eyes, perfectly able to navigate the pieces of glassware, cookbooks, bad photos of me and Ellis that his parents have framed and gifted to us, stacks of batteries, labeled boxes, hard drives, etc. stored above. He touches a potted plant at the ledge of the window at the kitchen sink (are these the first leaves he's ever touched?), then scampers directly toward us. Harris falls out of the way.

"Sig!" I call out. I try to catch him, but he brushes past my legs, tickling my bare ankle with the end of his tail.

Sig bounds into the street, barely making it past a car whipping around the bend. It's dusk, and everything outside is a shade of blue. I can just make out his shape as he darts across the rest of the road. He doesn't turn to survey us, to see if we'll follow him into the brush that lines the other side of the street. He springs up onto an azalea bush and disappears within.

18

Samir and I spend a few chagrined hours looking for Sig. We search under cars, shine a flashlight's wavering beam into the airy crown of every sycamore tree in a five-block radius of my house. We call his name. Then I call the names of some of the marmoset researchers in case they're familiar to him and might evoke some fond memories or special attachments.

"Tingwei, Dayo!" I shout.

"Do you know what kind of research they're doing with him?"

I don't.

"Those might be people he'd avoid," Samir says.

We continue our sweep of the neighborhood, but Sig never appears. All we see are a stray cat and two squirrels chattering as they high-wire a wood-post fence.

Around midnight, we return to my house. I wash my hands of the marshmallow sugar that has melted in my damp palms and then offer Samir a beer in the hopes that he might stay over. I add that Ellis is in San Diego until the end of the week.

Samir stands by the door with his sneakers on. I try to read his face, but it's impossible.

"I'm going to pretend I was never here," he says after a while. "I never saw any of this. I don't know anything."

Still, he stands at the threshold of the door, not moving. I pour the beer into a glass anyway. Isn't this our little ritual? This ebb and flow, will we or won't we, should we or shouldn't we? I regret my outburst earlier. My display of needing clarity from him. Clarity has never been the point. Clarity will result in our decisive separation. Uncertainty is our lifeblood.

Samir stares at the glass. I can tell that he's weighing things now, evaluating. His hair is greasy, blade-like. He's quiet for a moment. His eyes are sunken but calculating.

"I'm sorry I got you involved," I say finally. "I'll figure it out myself." I put my palms up in a little faux surrender.

"Right," Samir says.

Casually, I open the fridge, survey its contents, and close it again. I repeat that he can stay a little longer if he'd like, but he declines.

"Back to Sora's house," I say. Samir makes no movement. He mentions Sora so rarely that I used to sometimes think, with hope, that he had broken up with her and not told me.

That he was making grand, if hidden, plans for us to be together.

Samir opens the door, which gets caught on the area rug, and fits himself through the small gap it allows. A huge, orange moon hovers just above the shrub line that banks Harris's yard. Pale ears of fungus sprouting from a pile of logs cast mini black shadows on the grass. I am possessed by an impulse to grab Samir, not to let him go.

Instead, I ask him not to tell anyone about what's happened. "I'll sort it all out. I'll find Sig. I'm sorry I even bothered you about it."

He says not to worry and that he'll see me tomorrow.

After I'm sure he's gone, I go outside and pour the remaining raisins in a snaking trail down the driveway.

I call Ellis, and we talk for a bit. Apparently, the airline misplaced his bag, so he had given his talk wearing a very large UCSD T-shirt from the campus store. "Felt kind of like a power move, if I'm being honest."

Laughing feels good, if precarious.

"What about you?" he asks. "You okay? Your day all good?"

I can't bear to bring up the evening's events. I feel too shaky for Ellis's distinctly paternalistic brand of reproach/advice, however loving and well intentioned it is. Instead, I press him for details about the conference, how his talk was received.

There was a time when Ellis and I told each other everything. Or it felt like we did. Thoughts occurred to us, and we would say them. No filters, no lag.

We told each other about our triumphs and failures in lab, of a shitty day's arc, of plotlines from nonsensical dreams. Lost pets, old lovers spotted in coffeeshops, aromas that transported us suddenly to childhood, grudges we still harbored against family and friends. This was how we dealt our love to one another. Ellis and I heard it all—like lesser gods hearing infinite prayers, like gentle pets hearing the secrets of needful children.

Not that the telling was special, I always thought. Telling each other everything meant little more than garden-variety narcissism, a puerile need to be seen, heard, and validated. It was the listening that mattered. The listener's love and sense of duty, the listener's interest in the mundane, the listener's forgiveness of irrational and repetitive thinking. It was the care with which the listener handled the talker's dullest thoughts and ideas.

Wasn't it? Now, I can't be sure. Is this really what I think love should sound like? Silence?

I recite the details of Ellis's flight to Newark Airport where I will pick him up the following week.

"My only request is that you take rush hour into account," Ellis says. "As you know—"

I interject with a saying of his father's that we like to poke fun at, "Early is on time."

We laugh, say we love each other, and hang up.

That night, I'm sure I'll dream of her. For once, I want to. Everything I've done today would merit her unequivocal condemnation, and it's an odd comfort to think of that head of hers, floating toward me, rolling its eyes in frank disapproval. A vision I'd understand, for once. One that would require no deciphering. But no one appears in my dreams at all, and I sleep rather peacefully through the night.

19

Penny calls me the next morning before I've even gotten into the shower.

"Was it Samir?" I ask her. "Did he say something to you?"

"Are you fucking out of your mind?"

I scan my mind for the right tone and words of contrition, but nothing particularly compelling comes to mind. "Sorry," I say flatly.

Penny threatens to send Sinai security to my house in search of the missing marmoset. She doesn't believe me when I tell her that Sig has run away. "What the hell is going on with you," she hisses into the phone. "He's a body of research. Years of research. Get a dog if you're so starved for affection."

I reiterate that I no longer have any idea where he is. When I ask if she wants me to come into lab, she hangs up the phone.

Days pass in an uneasy haze. I walk the entire neighborhood with marshmallows in my pockets. I sleep with the windows open and leave bowls of nuts and raisins on the ledges. I stop short of posting LOST PET signs on tree trunks and telephone poles, not wanting to provoke Harris or any other neighbors to spread rumors about me. Every morning there is evidence that the bowls of food have been tampered with, but none to suggest that it was Sig.

. . .

The security office had combed through a few hours of footage and found a clip (which Penny forwarded to me) of me leaving the fourth-floor lab with a marmoset tucked in the crook of my elbow. The video clarity is so high that you can see the gentle movement of my fingers as I rub and tickle Sig behind the white tufts of hair, under his chin. I watch and rewatch myself coax him into my coat pocket and wave a blameless goodbye to Tingwei and the others on the second floor.

Needless to say, I am asked not to return to Sinai. Even Ellis, with his NIH money, cannot (and will not) defend me. At Sinai's behest, he terminates my employment contract and ferries home a nondisclosure agreement for me to sign, as well as a bill for the lost lab animal.

Ellis reports the gossip that circulates about me with tentative laughter, but I can feel him watching me. I suppose I seem crazy to him and everyone. Whatever reputation I once had is destroyed. People are no longer worried that I'm incompetent or accident-prone, but that I might return to harm animals or other people in the lab.

The night I sign the NDA, Ellis pours himself a glass of wine and points the bottle's nose toward me, offering me some. I accept and hold the glass without drinking from it.

"I had to talk down some rumors that you're part of a PETA operation," he says.

"You can ply me with wine, but I won't reveal our secrets."

A row of Ellis's straight, small teeth appears and then disappears again. He gives me a sidelong look. "I've also had to reassure people that you weren't going to kill yourself."

"Whoever thought that doesn't know me very well."

Ellis scoffs at this. "To be fair, you're behaving strangely, so people don't know what to think."

"Are you people?"

"Just help me understand what's going on with you."

But even I barely understand. If I did, I could reason myself out of it. I wouldn't be staring down the barrel of unemployment and a $3,500 bill from Sinai.

I've certainly tried to figure it out. For days, I summoned all the feeble explanations I could think of. That I wanted to sabotage the marmoset lab, that I was drawn to Sig by maternal instinct, that I felt a duty to protect God's creatures. I compared each possibility with the other, but none of them were true or made any sense.

"I just felt like I had to," I answer. "Like there was no other choice. But I can't trace where that impulse came from. He sort of communicated it to me."

"He. The marmoset." Ellis can commute his disdain with the simple rise and fall of an eyebrow.

"Yes, sort of." I sit down, suddenly very tired. "Well, I'm not explaining it right." I fumble a bit for something else to say, but my heart isn't in it.

"Maybe it's not that complicated, Len. Maybe people who don't take responsibility for themselves do random things they can't explain."

"That's not a very generous reading of my behavior."

He gives me a flinty stare. "Okay, then give me another way to read it. Explain it to me so I understand."

"But it's the explaining that I'm tired of. It doesn't get us anywhere. The expounding, the justifying, the defending. What is it for? So that we have a story to tell each other?" I move past Ellis, hold a lowball glass under the faucet. "Isn't it possible that some things within us just can't be explained? We contain multitudes, et cetera?"

"Sure, yes, but you can share these multitudes, can't you?" Ellis follows me into the kitchen. "I know it hasn't been an easy year. No one would blame you for saying so."

"It hasn't been an easy year," I chant. "It hasn't been an easy year." I'm joking, but the words pain me enough that I have to turn away from him. I drain my glass and fill it again. I make a racket with the ice tray.

"Just tell me the truth," Ellis says. He tugs at a loose thread in the wrist of his sleeve. "I can handle anything, but I need to hear it from you. I just don't know where you are anymore." The tenderness in his voice, in his whole person, threatens to unravel me.

He presses his wine-dark lips together. "Harris came by today. He wanted me to know that a quote-unquote young-looking, brown-skinned guy was in our house late on the night that our marmoset ran away."

My face produces a horrible little smile. "Is Harris the neighborhood watch now?"

"Be serious, Eleanor," he says.

Hypocrisy roils the pit of my stomach. Bile rises in me and hooks at my throat, but I hold perfectly still. I do not react. Imagine the pale belly of a fish or frog that appears on the water's surface. Imagine a leaf that skates on the wind and floats silent to the forest floor.

He says my name again.

"You were away." I shrug before Ellis's hand can reach my shoulder. "So I asked Samir to come over and help me with Sig. He left within the hour."

This is all true, of course. Things can be simple if only you let them.

Striving and Spoiled

Jing called Narisa to the office the following week. It was a yellowed trailer extension whose interior smelled and looked like wet cardboard.

"No more working beside the laborers," he said. "You'll be the boss one day. You can't sit around spitting and laughing with them."

Earlier that morning, he had emerged from the office to find his daughter tying neat bows alongside the workers, making jokes in her loud, bad Chinese, and waiting for Peng or Minru or Shan to laugh politely.

"I was getting to know them," said Narisa.

"If they respect you, they don't need to know you."

He tasked her instead with some low-impact administrative duties. Narisa answered the phone, she took messages.

She refilled the printer with paper and ink. She sharpened the pencils. She filed papers and pored through teen magazines looking for popular trends. She sorted binders by client name and swept up stray wig hairs that had fallen to the floor.

At lunchtime, Narisa sat in silence listening to the sound of her father supping from a Styrofoam bowl of soup or working over a tough piece of meat. Afterward, he drove off to make deliveries in the city, and Narisa returned to the warehouse floor to converse in her badly accented Mandarin with Jiajia and Peng. "Am I saying it right?" She flashed a flirtatious smile.

To be liked by the workers was useful, wasn't it? How else to get their attention? To hold sway when her father was delivering merchandise in the city most days? "Little Boss," they called her in Chinese, which was both an insult and a term of great and growing affection.

Only Minru stared blankly at the girl's attempts to warm them to her. She was wary of the children of Americanized immigrants, who were paradoxically striving and spoiled. Dangerous children. They were born of people who had become wealthy by running away from home.

"Ai, come on." Peng waved her hard words away. "Don't be so hard on us migrants. You didn't run away. Don't think of it that way. Think of yourself as a pioneer. Think about the life your son will have because of you."

"Don't talk about my son," Minru said.

Peng nodded. He rubbed the arthritic lump forming at the joint between the tip of his index finger. "What about my

Jiajia? Would you mistrust her, too? She's the daughter of an immigrant, is she not?" he said. "And I grow more American every day. It can't be helped." Lately he had been eating those boxed wheat ears, for example, slathered in cow's milk and yellow dust that formed a mucous called cheese.

Minru laughed, tilting her head at Peng's daughter. Poor motherless child. The girl picked dried globules of craft glue from the surface of the table across the way. "Not her," Minru said. "Her children. I will mistrust her children someday."

. . .

Minru liked this Peng from Yiwu, but she was not above passing her judgments on him as well. "He should beat her into talking," Minru whispered more than once to Shan, whom she didn't like very much but who was the only other Chinese speaker with whom she could discuss Peng's parental deficiencies.

"He's too gentle," Shan agreed. "Even Boss doesn't treat his daughters with such softness."

"Well, Boss Jing takes his cue from the big boss of the family." Minru smirked. "That shrew wife of his."

But Shan didn't dare agree with that. She gave Minru a prim line of a smile and returned to her work. (This was why Minru never much enjoyed chatting with Shan, of course. She was a coward and had no sense of humor.)

Jiajia, who sat nearby, smiled to herself but did not look up. How often people talked about her and her father as if she weren't sitting right beside them! Somehow they were always forgetting that, though she did not speak, she could hear and understand them perfectly. They signed and signaled to her as if she were deaf or dumb, and she encouraged them by nodding at their gesticulating hands and their short, repeated commands.

Her teeth were small white kernels stuck in a gummy smile, and she was often pressing on her round cheeks, as if she hoped to deflate them. It was this daft aspect of Jiajia's that made people think she couldn't understand what they said.

Though she didn't speak, Jiajia did make noises, which could startle people. They thought her silence ought to be consistent. They wanted to rely on it. Perhaps this is why it was so appalling to them that she smacked and belched when she ate. That her laugh was a kind of barking sound. And early in spring, she discovered she was allergic to certain American trees, and each sneeze of hers was preceded by a nasal little shout, "Hehhh-choo."

Jiajia did follow her father's orders (cleaned their dishes after dinner; washed their clothes in the noisy, banging machine; and draped them to dry on the long Ethernet cable that served as the clothing line in their room), but it turned out Jiajia was neither shy nor deeply pious, as Narisa and many of the workers had initially thought. She played little pranks (stole thread, unplugged hot glue guns). She laughed quite loudly when Peng waggled his ears at her or presented to her some new and American oddity—a hollow egg shaped chocolate at Easter or a long cane of fried, sugar-dusted dough. Some nights, she could even be heard crying, but in the morning she was always herself again.

She simply did not speak. She had not spoken since her mother had fallen down the elevator shaft of the last warehouse (a hulk of a building on a massive campus in Yiwu) and she would not speak for many years into her life in America. (When she finally did, the soft pitch of her voice and the loose curl of her accent would pleasantly surprise her.)

. . .

Jiajia was dazzled by the older girl who had entered the warehouse that spring. She paid careful attention to Narisa's perfect English and the athleticism with which she cleaned, swept, moved about the warehouse. One morning, she found herself staring at Narisa as she used their shared bathroom mirror to apply makeup and blow her long hair dry in mesmerizing, rhythmic motions.

Narisa turned to Jiajia and gave her a broad toothy smile. "Want try?" she asked in her American accent. "Come here." Narisa patted shimmery dust onto Jiajia's eyelids and lined the girl's eyes with black liquid whose bottle guaranteed it would not smudge or lighten for the rest of the day. "You're so pretty," Narisa said as she used a soft brush to put the finishing touch on Jiajia's cheeks.

Jiajia looked into the mirror. The black eyeliner gave her a sleepy, unimpressed look, and the powder made her gray like a ghost. But she gave her cousin a wide, grateful smile.

She had met older boys and girls at the factory in Yiwu, but they were no one to admire. Narisa moved about the warehouse with such confidence, such coolness. Her thin, penciled eyebrows were always arched just so, and was it a defect of the jaw or was Narisa constantly jutting her chin out in disapproval of everyone but Jiajia herself? Was it money that made her so languid? English? How else to explain it? She was just so American. She even had that wide-jawed smile. Always ready for a photograph, prepared to present a glistening fence of white teeth.

Little Boss was a good influence on Jiajia, Peng thought as he watched his girl's eyes following Narisa. She seemed kind and sisterly. She brought the girl chips and snacks from the vending machines in the warehouse across the parking lot and chattered to her in that rapid, watery English, which would surely be good for Jiajia once she began going to school (though he was still undecided on when that would be). Sometimes she dressed Jiajia in the sample headbands and heavy costume jewelry.

"Walk like y'got a plate on the head," Narisa would suggest in her butchered Mandarin. "Graceful. Like a model."

And Jiajia did. The lines of her arms broke at the wrist, where she held her palms parallel to the ground and modeled the goods down a runway Narisa had made, lined with cardboard boxes and packaging plastics.

Jiajia had one outfit that she wore most often—a yellow sweat suit with a cartoon rabbit embroidered on the back. And when Narisa got tired of seeing it, she asked Eleanor to collect and bring all the clothes they both had outgrown. Same with their old books, elementary school primers, toys Jiajia might like, sneakers, coats, hats. Jiajia accepted any item the sisters gifted her. She wore the old clothes indiscriminately, regardless of season or style.

"That look nice," Narisa would say of a pilled sweater that Jiajia draped over her shoulders.

It was a smooth symbiosis. Jiajia was grateful to have a friend, and Narisa happy to cast her old things off to someone as appreciative and wide-eyed as Jiajia.

Eleanor found these charitable exchanges, and the fashion shows that ensued, very embarrassing. Wasn't Narisa basically forcing Jiajia to wear these clothes? To be in a constant state of gratitude about all that Narisa was bestowing upon her? They lived in the same space after all; they shared a wall, a bathroom. How could Jiajia do anything but express her utmost appreciation for whatever Narisa gifted her?

When Eleanor raised her concerns, Narisa tipped her head in the way she always did when she was dismissing someone. "Remind me never to accept a gift from you," she said.

But Narisa *did* accept gifts from Eleanor. Or had she already forgotten? Eleanor had visited the warehouse almost every afternoon that month, bearing treats purchased with the allowance she had begun to receive from her parents. Pizza, which was sold by the slice every Wednesday afternoon at the entrance to the basketball gym. Cans of Veryfine juice from the machine at the Judaica warehouse across the street.

Sometimes, if Eleanor read a book in English class that she thought might suit Narisa's interests, she would swipe it after the unit was over and bring it to the warehouse for Narisa to read.

Narisa gave little indication as to whether she enjoyed these novels, but she at least offered evidence that she had read them, which satisfied Eleanor. She called *The Little Prince* "depressing, but I'd read the sequel." *Lord of the Flies* was "melodramatic." She handed *The Bluest Eye* back to Eleanor without a word, and when Eleanor pressed for a response, Narisa only said: "I don't want to talk about it."

Eleanor nodded. She understood. She and Narisa never spoke openly about anything. Why would they start now? Eleanor saw these books less as fodder for conversation and more as a kind of code they could use. Perhaps seeing and reading the same words would bring the girls closer than their scant communications ever could.

•   •   •

It was a gray, windy spring during which there seemed always to be a storm brewing, though one never arrived. March was a slow month at the warehouse, and Narisa grew restless. She began taking her bike out in the afternoons, which Minru scoffed at. Everyone else tried simply to appear busy for fear that Jing might look out onto the floor and decide to let one or two of them go (as he had done last year around this time).

Narisa made long, inertial loops around old points of interest—the wood chip playground, the high school basketball courts, Raymond's Deli. All the places that had dotted the map of her life just two months earlier.

She rode by the park where she and her friends used to smoke or light leaves and other little objects on fire. From the other side of the park, she could see them. Their bookbags were strewn on the rotted picnic table with the missing bench. Lora's mouth gaped with laugher as she tied her hair into two loose coils, like ears on either side of her head. CJ's wide-legged pants whipped in the wind, exposing the outline of his long, twiggy legs. Lily smiled, but without looking up from the joint she was rolling in her lap.

Narisa rode past once, then twice, then turned and rode past again. If they saw her, they gave no indication that they did. She wanted desperately to say hi, to sit and joke around, to watch the whorls of smoke reveal the direction of the wind. But she couldn't bring herself to ride up to the fence.

What would she do, she thought, as she followed the sidewalk along the canal, past the elementary school, through the neighborhood of identical stuccoed houses? Could she see herself working here with her father for the rest of her life? She had never really asked herself what she could envision for her life or where it might lead.

A dense layer of clouds had obscured the sunlight all day. How could you tell what time of day it was when the light stayed the same shade of gray from morning to afternoon? She kept riding. Another loop around the neighborhood, and another. She would have ridden around again, had a voice not called to her as she passed by the deli for a fifth time.

"Are you stalking me?" A boy with minnowy eyes and a no-nonsense haircut sat on a bench outside of the deli. He bit into a wet sandwich. Liquid dripped onto the paper plate below.

"No." Narisa clipped her voice as she always did around strangers, but she slowed her bike to a stop.

"You lost, then?"

"No."

"Third time I've seen you since I was sitting here."

"Does it take that long to eat a sandwich?"

"I'm on my break." He gestured behind him at the deli, then balled the paper wrapper of his sandwich into a pellet and lobbed it toward the trash can. "Shit." He sprang to grab it as it bounced away. "I normally make it." The boy laughed at himself, stooped to collect the wrapper.

He wore yellow basketball shorts, white basketball shoes, a black basketball jersey with the insignia of a man palming a basketball. Sparse black hairs shaded his legs. He had bulbous calves and bony ankles.

"You want something from inside? A Coke?" The boy looked to be about Narisa's age. Maybe sixteen or seventeen. Pale freckles constellated underneath his eyes.

"No, thanks," Narisa said. What was the feeling she was having? Something was rising in her, threatening to spill over. She pedaled away.

. . .

The next day, Narisa returned to Raymond's at noon. She leaned her bike against the wooden table where the boy had been sitting and entered the deli.

Basketball boy was there. Behind the counter. He wore a dingy apron, gloves, and a Bulls cap, over which lay a set of black headphones, the kind that acted as low-grade speakers to everyone else. The boy lowered his head to an oversized sandwich, placing fine-sliced tomatoes on a slab of matte white cheese.

He was transfixed by this particular sandwich, bouncing to his music as he worked, and didn't notice Narisa standing in line, watching him. But he moved like he was being watched, like he hoped he was. Q-Tip spoke tinnily from the boy's headphones. Something dinged in the oven behind him, and he spun on his toes and slid toward it. On the ledge of the glass case was a glass jar on which he (or someone else) had written in marker: "Like what I do? $$"

This whole display at once attracted and embarrassed Narisa. She liked the way he moved, skated, bounced. She watched the sinews of his arms move and noted the dexterity of his hands—the way his thin fingers guided the work he was doing, not his palms or his arms.

"Meatball parm?" The boy wrapped and taped the sandwich with a flourish of the wrist. Narisa heard the faintest curl at the end of the word "ball." Korean, she thought.

A woman wearing jewel-green scrubs took the sandwich from his outstretched hands. "You all ain't got your own music?" she addressed him, and then looked to Narisa, too, as if she might speak on his behalf.

"No, ma'am, I guess we don't," he said, then thanked her for the bill she dropped into his jar.

Narisa's stomach gurgled from hunger and nerves as she approached the counter. She wanted to shake herself out of whatever fog was rendering her so thick-tongued and dumb. How did one order a sandwich? She smiled broadly when she saw him, but only because he was smiling so broadly at her. She stumbled over some sandwich words and then retracted them, leaving the shop empty-handed.

20

It's early. Not even dawn. The sky is just starting to hint blue, and jagged shapes of light appear between the tree leaves outside our bedroom window. Ellis breathes gently beside me. Careful not to wake him, I slip out from under our covers.

Today is another day of searching for Sig. As has been my routine this week, I circle Art Park, where I think it's most likely Sig would have run to. I train my eyes on the tree line and then systematically move down each of the park's curved, gravel pathways, making note of where and when I find root-shaped bits of feces. (Though I'm aware these might be the makings of some other creature. A toy dog, a raccoon.) Every ten feet or so, I drop a few peanuts and banana chips onto the path.

According to the Mount Sinai animal care guide, common marmosets are social animals who cannot tolerate living alone or in isolation. They have excellent memories, and for this reason, I hold on to the possibility that Sig will return to me, and that I can return him to the lab.

Many triumphant fantasies emerge during these search days of mine. Sig leaps onto my shoulder, and I take a picture of him, send it to Penny, who finds it funny and forgives me immediately. Or: Sig returns to my house through the flue of our unused fireplace, nuzzles against me, becomes my beloved pet. Or: In an absurd twist of events, Sig makes his way back to Mount Sinai, where the research on his body is invalidated but where he becomes some kind of social media mascot for his remaining years.

Or: Sig emerges from a line of hedges, speaks to me with my mother's voice. But what would the voice say? What revelation would mother-Sig bestow upon me? Even in my fantasy, I can't quite conjure it.

Where is she? I have been wishing my mother would disappear since I was a child. I wished for her death when I didn't understand what death was. I wished for her to be a kinder or gentler person when I didn't understand who she was. Later on, I wished for her to be happy, though I saw no way of guiding her there. And above all, I wished so many times that she would simply be quiet, muffle that voice of hers that rang in my ears, even when we were apart.

After she died, I genuinely thought that she might haunt me. She would be my ghost and hex everything I did. (Why should death change what she did in life?) But it isn't her haunting me; I understand that now. I am haunting her. Grabbing hold of her ghostly sleeves, the hems of her phantom dress. Seizing every word she's ever spoken. I can't let go. I'm afraid to.

*   *   *

It takes me just over three hours to comb the entire park. Gradually, my coat pockets empty of the sugared peanuts and banana chips I've filled them with. Unleashed dogs follow me, their owners trailing apologetically after them.

By noon, the pads of my feet ache. I walk to the shallow man-made lake where turtles paddle the surface or rest on thin logs with their heads raised to the sun. Behind me is a grove of trees, which I imagine might provide the best cover to a fearful animal in a strange place.

Facing the water, I sit on a bench and shed some private, requisite tears. My scientific career is over. I see that clearly now. Had my mother portended as much? Everything Ellis was, I would not be, she'd said. Was this what she had in mind?

I always thought I would return to the neuroscience program, even as I feigned indifference to encouragement from Ellis, Penny, and the others. Secretly and under some delusion, I believed that I would return in triumph. That I would prove to all those oversimplifiers and mediocre conclusion drawers—my mother the most vociferous among them—that one could take the long, circuitous route and still arrive alongside the others, if not ahead of them.

I see now that this was all a fantasy. That the defeated often confuse themselves for the resolute. We think we're just biding our time.

After my morning search, I return home and spend the remainder of the day occupied with various household tasks. Do laundry, vacuum the rugs, prepare dinner, sweep the porch. Between these tasks, I debate whether or not to get an abortion. I am trying to think clearly, but there's something wrong with my thinking altogether. I understand that I have decisions to make, but every coherent thought feels out of reach. Every day that passes invalidates the thinking I did the previous day. Each day the little bug in me becomes something else, develops some other aspect of her body and her brain. Am I to be a mother? As the days pass, I begin to feel certain of nothing else. Nothing but her inexorable arrival.

Rid Yourself of Pride

What did Narisa think about before there was Gabriel? she sometimes wondered. What had occupied her mind? Every day, Narisa counted all the things she loved about Gabriel: his odd freckles, his skinny brown ankles, the woody taste of his mouth. She imagined his hands while she sat at work, while she brushed her teeth, while she cleaned up after dinner. (Though she lived at the warehouse, Narisa continued to eat her dinners at home. Each night, Rita set a plate for Narisa and cooked enough rice for four but refused to speak to her most disappointing daughter during the meal.)

"He's kind of obsessed with me," Narisa told Eleanor, when she visited at the warehouse after school. Though the amount of time Narisa spent talking about him revealed to Eleanor that the obsession was, at least, mutual.

Gabriel had a car, and he could often be seen waiting outside of the warehouse for Narisa. If Eleanor was with her, she would climb into the back and let whatever music he played drown out their vapid conversation. She had learned not to involve herself in their affairs. (Narisa glared at her if she ever tried to contribute to the conversation.) But she did watch her sister. She had forgotten how playful Narisa could be. She fluttered and preened in the front seat. She pressed her forehead to the passenger window, leaned her head on Gabriel's shoulder. She shouted out to people walking the sidewalk, picked through the car's glove box and made fun of its contents.

After they dropped Eleanor off at home, she'd watch from the front window as they rolled down the street. She sometimes caught herself imagining the car turning into a white speck headed toward a vanishing point on the horizon, though in reality they always made the first left toward Gabriel's neighborhood and quickly disappeared from view.

Sometimes Rita was home and sometimes she was off shopping or taking photos or visiting at her friend Opera's house. Always, though, the house was warm with evidence that she had been there. A ruffled magazine on the kitchen counter, waterlogged bread crusts in the kitchen sink, fresh cigarette ends and toothpicks in the cut-glass ashtray.

Typically, when her mother was home, Eleanor holed herself up in her room until she was called to dinner. She did homework, she read. She might descend to the kitchen for an apple or a yellow square of plastic-wrapped cheese.

On days when no one was around, Eleanor was less dutiful. She could while away an entire afternoon exchanging messages with strangers on the family's desktop computer, which was tucked into an alcove by the living room. These conversations were routinely sexual and highly educative to Eleanor, who had, as of yet, no sexual knowledge aside from what she could glean from television and Narisa's occasional, cryptic hints.

In chat rooms Eleanor found she could hold two or three conversations simultaneously with a seemingly endless parade of usernames. Most conversations began with questions about her body: sizes, shapes, what could fit where, etc. and could carry on with minimal input on her part. She was quickly able to extrapolate, often copying what humannyc78 wrote, for instance, and pasting it into a conversation about what she would do with camel0t1616, if only they were together.

Rarely, some of the users asked her what she liked, but Eleanor did not know the answer to that. The very possibility of liking or disliking sex acts was beyond her comprehension. Like standing on the ridge of a dizzying mountain, in awe of the endless range, and having someone ask you which peak you prefer.

. . .

Gabriel's house was a large, egg-colored Victorian in a neighborhood filled with other large Victorians. Massive elm trees surrounded the houses, protecting the families from the inconvenience of having to see or interact much with one another. Willow trees draped and curtained themselves. Aging white pines threatened the cars that sat beneath them.

Gabriel's room (which he shared with his older brother, who was now away at college) took up the larger part of a high-ceilinged basement with plush, heathered carpets. The first time Gabriel invited Narisa to his home, they passed by a long mirrored bar behind which sat a phalanx of gleaming liquor bottles. Framed posters of race cars and nighttime cityscapes adorned the adjacent walls. A hammered gold cross drew the eye up and away from an unused fireplace.

"Who *decorated* this place?" Narisa played. Her stomach churned as she moved toward the couch, and she sat on her hands lest their shivering betray her nervousness. On the opposite wall was a poster of a Firebird parked puzzlingly within a grove of bluish green trees. Gabriel sat beside her, so close that Narisa's focus flitted among the parts of his face— from one pale iris to the other to the dark flesh of his mouth.

Narisa had seen enough TV to know how to lean in for a kiss. (Not to close the eyes or cartoonishly pucker the mouth, but to stare baldly and to part the lips just slightly. An invitation, a vulnerability.) But Gabriel didn't kiss her. He put a hand on her breast. They did not look at each other but at Gabriel's broad-nailed fingers, which curved around the side of Narisa's body, down her ribs and then settled at the crevice between her hip and thigh. The other hand traveled a similar path, and Narisa, not knowing where to look, closed her eyes.

. . .

That year, Rita watched her daughter and fretted (as her own mother had fretted about Rita, who had always been guileless around men and boys, unable to hold herself still, to train herself into silence). She wanted badly, guiltily, for her daughter to go somewhere, anywhere. To join the army or move in with a friend who had wealthy, well-meaning parents.

Look at this daughter sashaying about the house, as if gliding through water. What reason did a girl have to smile so much? Only one that Rita knew of. And the way she smiled—not to herself, but outwardly, opening like a flower. Did the girl's hips seem wider? Her breasts larger? Or was it all in Rita's mind? Sex was either here, or it loomed dark on the horizon, she thought.

"What is it?" Rita pressed her daughter that night. It was the first time she had addressed Narisa directly in weeks. She folded the family's clothes while Narisa watched a muted television show. Eleanor sat in the large round chair by the piano. Her legs and arms folded at the knees and elbows, all extremities meeting at one central location: her book. Like a spider working over an ant.

"Hmm?" Narisa looked up.

"You've been acting strange," Rita said. She laid Jing's shirt to her body, using her chest as a board to fold clothes against.

"Maybe I am strange," Narisa said. But she couldn't hide that distant, contented look in her eye as if she had found a clear and secret lake to swim in.

"Is there something special going on?" asked Rita.

"No." Narisa tilted her head, tried but failed to suppress a smile.

"No?" Rita sidled. "Tell me," she said.

Eleanor rolled her eyes from where she sat, watching her mother and sister circle each other above the edge of her book. She hated them. Their bad acting, their caginess. Why did her mother ask questions she knew the answers to? Why couldn't Narisa suppress anything of herself, not even a damn smile? She could not stomach this interaction and retired upstairs to her room.

Remove yourself from this scene for a moment. Imagine a mother and child who are friends.

Come on, the mother might play. *Is there a boy in your life?*

Narisa might give her mother a conspiratorial look, a playful flip of her long hair. *If there were, I wouldn't tell you!*

Imagine a mother whose grasp of English was not simply a mastery of vocabulary, that circuitous grammatical structure— all those singular, plural conjugations, those masculine, feminine pronouns, the endless verb tenses for things past, things distant past, things to come, things that happen, things that are happening. Imagine a mother who knew not only all of these Byzantine rules but also the unspoken ones. Chinese cleverness is full of homonyms, wordplay, but how does a Chinese woman learn the tone of wisecracking, sarcasm? In America, insolence is a form of love. How was Rita to know all that?

"Come here," Rita said.

Narisa unfolded her limbs, stood and padded over to her mother, stared at her pink nose.

Rita looked at her daughter. That narrow, wasting face. Was this the daughter she had raised? She searched Narisa's face for some sign. Of what? Of herself. Of Jing. Of Eleanor. Of something or someone she could recognize. The tip of her nose burned.

A few days earlier, while doing the girls' laundry, Rita had found a stain in Eleanor's underwear. Muted brown blood. And only then had it occurred to her that Narisa had never gotten her period. Or, more likely, that the girl had hidden it from her. Why, why, why? Why did these girls do anything?

Over the years, Rita had gained such little knowledge of her daughters' interior lives. They had grown into volatile, dreaming girls who behaved sometimes as if their eyes were closed, or turned inward toward unknowable things. What would they be like when they were grown? Where did they plan to go? She knew from the way they moved about the world—Narisa: roving and wraith-like, Eleanor: stiff and watchful—that they belonged elsewhere.

To another mother, this opacity may have been concerning. But where Rita was exacting in certain areas, she was forgiving in others. She had no interest, she told herself, in knowing the landscape of her daughters' hearts and minds. Why should she know them? What made her so deserving? She sought only to govern their behavior, not their thoughts, those dark spaces she would never see.

Rita had summoned Narisa to her but could not bring herself to press on with interrogating her. She collected herself and pointed at a mound of laundry. "Be useful."

Narisa surveyed the mixed pile of socks and wrinkled shirts. "None of this is mine."

"Impudent," Rita said, tasking her daughter to the pile again.

That night at dinner, Rita assessed her daughters. Eleanor ate so close to her bowl that the tip of her nose might graze the rice. She watched Narisa for some expression of satisfaction, some indication that the decision to send her to work had been the right one. Perhaps Narisa was just the kind of girl who preferred to be useful, preferred to work. (Rita herself had been that way as a teenager.) But Rita could never make anything out of her daughter's blank stare.

Jing had said that Narisa was happy working, but what did he know about a woman's happiness? Rita watched her daughter spoon a heap of braised eggplant onto her plate. Seated at the dinner table, she was sullen and averted her eyes when the others spoke. Her silence felt to Rita like a direct and punishing rebuke.

"How much longer do you plan to live among those illegal workers?" Rita asked. She picked at a bit of dried food stuck to the end of her fork.

"Maybe until they kick me out for wasting the bathwater," said Narisa.

Eleanor cringed. Why did Narisa say things she knew she shouldn't? She looked to her mother, but it was Jing who grabbed Narisa's wrists, as if he planned to stand her up and box with her. He twisted her arms and threw her out of her chair. Narisa's fork clattered somewhere on the floor.

"Liu Jing," Rita cried. She fell beside her daughter, putting a hand on the back of the girl's head.

Eleanor remained where she was. The key, she'd discovered, was not to move or respond when he got like this. Not to scream or cry out, not to draw attention. She sat with her back straight against the chair. The key was not to avoid his eyes either, but to look at him like you couldn't recognize who he was.

"Listen to me," he said to Narisa, who was hunched beside her mother like a small rounded bug. "Rid yourself of pride before you come back to this house."

.   .   .

Narisa gritted her teeth as she rode her bike to Gabriel's. Pride, what pride? She let the wind cool her burning face. What did the word mean to them? They used the word "pride," but they meant "self." They wanted her to disappear, to replace herself with someone who obeyed, who made herself into fine grains of sand that could fit into any box or bottle they presented. They wanted another Eleanor. Another daughter who had no self but theirs.

But the more they pressed her to contort herself into something that they wanted, the more Narisa hated them for it. There was nothing here for her. She understood that now. She would make her plans. She would leave them.

A Shallow Hole in the Yard

It would have been better for Rita if she had just accepted that Jing would never love her. What they had was a partnership— a peaceful and profitable one built on mutual interests, which Rita had convinced even herself that they shared.

This was nothing tragic, Rita's friend Opera counseled. Hadn't love grown from much less fertile grounds than a thriving business and a three-bedroom house overlooking the water? Maybe, Rita thought. But her tenacious pursuit of Jing was beginning to falter. In three years of marriage, nothing organic had developed. Nothing had come into being between her and Jing that she herself had not carefully arranged.

They had sex, though infrequently. Jing pummeled at something deep and unreachable inside Rita, and Rita spread herself open as far as she could. She put her hands on his damp back and his laboring ass, in hopes of letting Jing farther and farther inside. Eventually, he would groan and spill himself into her, and she would close her legs feeling odd and unmoved. It wasn't the fault of her wandering mind or low libido, as one might think. Something in *him* resisted *her*, Rita thought. Try as she might, she could not swallow him whole.

Jing sensed, too, at least after sex, that Rita was never spent or satisfied. But he was not certain that this qualified as his responsibility. Sometimes he might reach over to her and finger the tuft of hair that sprouted from between her legs. But this did not garner much response. She just lay there. The streetlamp outside cast a harsh yellow light into their room.

Still, Rita devoted herself to improving the situation. Alone in the bathroom, she took deep, meditative breaths and examined the folds of her body. During sex, she tried to fantasize. She thought about strange men, lovely, aggressive women. She tried to recall the feeling of sexual want, of the suffocating privation she had felt when she had written to Jing from Taipei. That version of her had penned letters full of mawkish yearning and desperate pleas, but another Rita had carved and whittled at the letters until only a third Rita remained—wooden and bereft.

But simply recalling an earlier version of herself did not revive it. Wantful Rita had thrilled at having received the dubious letter from Jing (which turned out to be from his sister) inviting her to join him in New York (for a price). That Rita had snubbed her mother's disapproval. She'd been so sure of herself, fueled by the desperate belief that Jing would or at least could love her. That belief seemed to propel the very engine of the plane that carried her across the Pacific Ocean. It stimulated every atom in her being, every atom in the world, pulsated and pushed them toward this horizon, a life with Jing in America.

Where were all those feelings now? It was as if some tide had pulled in and then gone, taking parts of her with it out to sea. The business grew and stabilized. Rita prepared dinner for Jing each night and sometimes for Mindy and Hong, who came by often to visit.

What had she expected? she thought to herself. Where had she gotten these notions of romance? Of love so easily and equally reciprocated? Had she read about it in a book somewhere, or taken some childhood fairytale to heart? What was it that made her believe she deserved such love from Jing? Possibly a radio commercial. Or something extrapolated from the American and British music that trickled into the record collections at Wang's music store on Yongkang Street. She remembered the dim listening booth with startling clarity. It sometimes appeared in her dreams. A glitch of a memory: spartan wood paneling, the door that never latched shut for all the fabric that was glued around it.

Rita would understand later. After the girls were born. After they began to listen, to read, to watch, to observe. You could not know what went into a mind, which memories seared themselves in and which were eroded by the daily stimulations of living, working, caring, mothering. You could not know this about your own mind, either.

. . .

They became very casual with contraceptives. That is, Jing did, and Rita did not object. It rather excited him. He spilled himself into her night after night. Why shouldn't he? Rita was the one who worked into every conversation that she was of childbearing age. That each day that passed further disqualified her from it.

Jing thrilled at the thought of creating a child with Rita. Everything they did together went perfectly. She was his lucky, glittering charm. Everything she touched turned to gold, or some mechanism that spooled it. Were he a more superstitious man (or a woman), he thought, he might have suspected that he had been visited by a witch, a goddess. Those half-living creatures who could offer a man's wildest dreams but who could take them away just as swiftly. His fingertips were covered in ribbon dye and dried glue, but still she licked them at night in their bed.

. . .

After Narisa was born, Rita ceded almost all of her responsibilities at the warehouse. By this time, most RFPs were funneled to Liu Enterprises through referral anyway. And now that Jing's English and confidence had improved, Rita was not much needed at trade shows or new client meetings. She did continue to do the accounts from home, since she and Jing both agreed they could trust no one else to the task.

It was during this time of relative stability that Jing began traveling back to Taiwan every year to visit family, meet with suppliers, and establish Ah Mao as a partner in the business. At home before his departure, Jing and Rita would decide which gifts to give to which family members, how much cash to parcel out to their parents. Jing would prevail upon his sister to take care of Rita if she needed any help while he was gone, but Mindy never appeared, and Rita never called to ask for a helping hand.

Rita found she enjoyed this time she had to herself. Truly, it was the first time she felt she had ever been alone. Yes, there was Narisa to love and take care of. But caring for Narisa was not like looking after her siblings or fulfilling her duties as a wife. Narisa was a part of Rita, some vital appendage, whose happy functioning was essential to Rita's own. The daily chores and exertions of care were exhausting, but they satisfied her. There was rarely any question of what needed to be done. Never any uncertainty about the absolute necessity of Rita's care and protection.

And then there was the girl's attention and obsession to revel in. Was there anything so perfectly and painfully mutual as the compulsive need between a mother and her baby? Without the looming shadow of Jing returning from the warehouse each night, days and nights with Narisa stretched languidly into one another. Narisa slept and ate when she felt like it, and so did Rita. Some days, Narisa's cries of joy and distress (and Rita's answers to them) were all that punctuated the hours.

. . .

That year, Rita dug a shallow hole in the yard. She worked slowly, digging a bit each day whenever Narisa took one of her fitful naps. The hole was too short to be a grave. Too shallow to bury anything valuable.

She did not bring it up, and Jing did not ask about the small mound of dirt in their yard when he returned. Actually, he pretended he hadn't seen it. At night, he told a droopy-eyed Narisa stories about Taipei. The skin-like layers you could pull off the trunks of paperbark trees. The mangoes that dangled from lush, low branches behind the village he had lived in. All you had to do was shake a branch and these things would fall. Life was everywhere. And here? Life seemed to be nowhere. Even the canal, which they looked out onto every morning, was unnaturally still.

A week later, Rita put the earth back where it had come from. Her love for Jing. She buried it. She did not need it. She dressed herself back in that old lie. Jing was but a means to get herself to America, and she had made it. A week after that, Eleanor was born.

How life flew by then. The children, their needs, their hands grabbing at everything, desiring everything. Their desires replacing those of Jing and Rita. For some time, Jing courted women he met at the supermarket, women he saw in bars. If one—just one—had curled her finger at him, had asked him to (do what?), he would have. But no one ever did. They were charmed by him, they thought him sweet, they admired his smooth, jet-black hair. But when he hinted, ever so subtly, that he wanted them, they disappeared.

Gradually, he let this dream go. Dreamers can be volatile. They will drop what doesn't work for them. They will abandon that which doesn't serve them. But quitters, too, have sudden changes of heart. Abandoned hope lies always in wait. This was a dangerous time to be Jing's wife.

21

Are we good again? Are Ellis and I resolved? I know we haven't bared our hearts to one another in a long time, but we are actually functioning quite well these days. He doesn't ask me where I go each morning, and I don't ask him how things are at the lab. The distance makes way for a kind of grace between us.

We have been climbing back to where we were. Maybe even beyond where we were. My total adoption of the household chores has been seamless, if slightly penitent, as if a clean home and a square meal on the table each evening will cure whatever ails us. And maybe it will.

I have not seen or attempted to contact Samir, and if Ellis has spoken to him at work, he doesn't tell me anything about it. He seems aware of our recovery, too.

We're in the baked goods aisle contemplating our bread needs when I finally tell Ellis I'm pregnant. I can't hold it back any longer. It's a loaf of challah on one of the lower shelves, so bulbous and fertile, that does me in. Ellis lets out a shout of joy, hugs me over the shoulders.

"I knew it," he says twice and laughs into my hair. "I feel like I could just tell. God, you're so . . ." He holds a palm to my belly though there's nothing to feel but my underwear elastic digging at my waist. "I know things have been off lately, but it all makes so much sense." He kisses me. Shoppers navigate their carts around us.

"How long have you known?"

"It's about nine weeks along, I think."

His face falls a little bit, and I add quickly, "I just wanted to be sure before I told you."

"You already saw the doctor? Without me?"

"I didn't want to give you wrong information."

Ellis nods, says in a mild voice, "It's all right to just need some time to think things through. But I can tell now that you have."

I stare stupidly at him for a moment. Has thinking ever led me through something and out some other end?

"We make a good partnership, don't we? We take care of each other." His chin touches down on my shoulder. "A man alone ain't got no bloody fuckin' chance," he enunciates.

"Who is that, Melville?" I ask.

"Hemingway."

I nod. I lean against him, eye level to the wiry hairs that scale the collar of his shirt. What do I care about a man alone? What I want to know about is a woman alone. What is a woman alone? I can't imagine her.

"We have to celebrate," he says. Ellis loves to celebrate, and I love that about him. We careen around the store for a while, picking up items for a sauce he wants to make for dinner. Massive cans of peeled tomatoes, golden onions, okra bound in plastic.

He pushes the cart ahead of me and keeps turning to catch my eye, as if to make sure I'm still there. The prolonged hunt for a certain brand of jarred artichoke hearts sends us both into a spiral of giggles and pantomiming.

At home, Ellis tells me not to lift a finger. He calls me his angel and turns on the television, then points at a puckered spot on the couch where he wants me to sit and rest.

In the kitchen I can hear him slicing, mincing, turning on the gas stove. The wall shelves are perfectly organized from all the cleaning I did after Sig's short stay. It's satisfying in a way, but it also gives me the feeling I'm in someone else's home. Where is the evidence (dust, skin, disarray) that I belong here? I sit stiffly and watch TV.

It felt good, at the store, to spread joy like that, to pass it back and forth like a ball. In that moment I'd been the author of Ellis's happiness, had made him smile and hint pink in the face. But now at home, I can feel her, in this very instant, slipping away from me. In telling Ellis about her,

I've made her ours, not mine. Soon, she will be the world's. I have spoken her, which means that I have given her away. A leaden sensation in my belly pulls me low. The feeling you get when you've done someone wrong, something that can't be undone.

I close my eyes and raise the volume of the television over the sound of the stovetop fan. Ellis bustles in the kitchen, laughs at one of the sitcom jokes. One short "ha." From my seat, I can hear the crackle of oil being fried in a pan. The heady smell of overbrowning garlic perfumes the air. Is it making me hungry or is it making me nauseous? I can't discern between the two. The smell grows until it overwhelms my nose, fills my mouth and throat. I grab my coat and say something about needing fresh air.

Outside, a bird trills. Denuded trees shudder in the wind. The car keys clink pleasantly in my pocket. My mother, my mother. What would she do if she were me? It's been impossible to imagine. But now, suddenly, I feel I am on the brink of knowing. A voice carries on the breeze, but I can't make out what it says.

The car is still warm from when we left it moments ago. I reverse out of the driveway and head toward the turnpike.

22

Snow dusts the brick path that leads to the front door of my mother's house. I park the car at the curb. One part of me expects to see her waving me into the open garage. Another part of me is surprised to see the house still standing at all, after my mind had tried so hard to will it to the ground.

I sit in Ellis's car for so long that the sky begins to darken. My phone vibrates madly, but I ignore it. Why answer the phone when I can't offer Ellis what he's looking for?

After a while, the first-floor windows of the house brighten with yellow light. Behind the sheer curtains, I can see a slender figure moving from room to room. I can even make out the billowing of the curtains as she moves past them.

But it's a man who answers my knock at the door. We stare at each other. His hair is streaked silver and limp with grease. He is thinner than I remember but still broad-bodied, shaped like an armoire. I remember his face less clearly. Did he always look like this? The skin of his nose is mottled with gray spots. His eyes are wilted at the corners.

"Yaa. Ziqin." My father pays me an inadequate pat on the shoulder of my coat. His mouth suggests a sort of closed smile, like he's savoring the feel of my name on his tongue. "I've been waiting for you. You come on this cold a day?" He shepherds me into the house, directs my attention to a pair of worn slippers by the mat on the floor. I brush the snow from my coat, then hang it on a rack by the window.

"Hi! Sister!" Jiajia greets me from the table behind the pony wall that separates the kitchen from the living room. A nest of black hair sits on her head. Her nose spreads across her face as she smiles at me. She looks from me to my father. "A long time has passed," she says.

"My daughter," his voice booms. "Finally. The child comes to take care of business. Only half a year after her mother has left."

"Died," I correct.

"Don't be crass." He moves toward the kitchen. "Have you eaten? Please sit." My father throws a careless hand toward the kitchen cabinetry. "Bowls are over there," he says, as if I'm the stranger.

. . .

I understand now that I've interrupted dinner. There are half-served dishes of food arrayed in the center of the table. Short ribs in congealed sauce, a half-eaten fish flayed to its spine. Slips of silk melon bathing in their own waters. Even with bowl and chopsticks in hand, I can't bring myself to eat any of it.

In the empty living room, the TV blares. Cigarette butts bloom from an ashtray. A small mound of sunflower seed shells sits on a spread of the *World Journal*. The television rattles with an infomercial for a vacuum, and its seller's enthusiasm quickly overwhelms ours. My father watches the demonstration with apparent interest. Jiajia adds another member to the pile of spent ribs glistening on a paper plate.

After dinner, we drink a turbid oolong that scrapes the back of my throat and dilates my attention. We don't answer each other's questions. I ask where his family is, and he leans to ash his cigarette into the tray on the coffee table. He asks me about work, and I shrug, pour him another cup of tea. Somehow, this feels natural, and I suspect we both are asking questions we don't care to know the answers to. Eventually, the vacuum seller reclaims our attention.

My eyes start to feel small and desiccated, portending a headache. Is it the fragrance of the meal? The warmth of the kitchen? Is he really here, my father, amid these seed hulls and cigarettes? Under the glass of the table, I can see his bare toes play against the edge of his slippers. I spent so many years telling people he was dead that I suppose I'd begun to believe the tragic fate I'd designed for him. Even Ellis thinks he died of an accident involving black ice and bald tires.

During a commercial, Jiajia passes us in the kitchen, then returns with a glass of juice. She's let her frizzy hair down, and it swings against her back as she moves.

"Sister." She moves her hand toward me but doesn't touch me. "I'm so happy to see you. I've missed you. Will you be staying overnight?"

"Yes, stay," my father says. "It's already late. Dangerous to drive in the snow."

Jiajia: "We haven't touched any of your mother's things. We left everything for you. Not because we didn't want to clean it up. But out of respect for you, you understand." Bright silver earrings dangle from the lobes of her ears. The familiar use of "we" does not escape my attention.

"Thanks." I try to calculate her age in my head. How old was she when she first arrived at the warehouse? If I'm twenty-six now, she must be twenty. My father, fifty-five. "I think I'll stay if it's not too much trouble."

My father lights another cigarette. It takes all my will not to stare at him, not to ask him what he's doing here. Had my mother contacted him without telling me? Written him a letter? I plumb my mind for memories of visits during which she might have talked about him, or more likely, about topics adjacent to him. But nothing comes to mind.

Commercials appear on the screen, and we watch them with labored interest. A rain-wetted truck climbs uneven terrain. A patty of ground meat drips pink juice. A college student is pleased with her free credit report.

. . .

Upstairs, in my old bedroom, I have seven messages from Ellis.

What's up Len?

Where are you?

You okay?

Don't freak out. I love you.

Please we're in this together.

Call me.

Test.

Test: the likelihood of a technical failure being more imaginable to Ellis than my ignoring him. Test: Does a person's patience run out or does it tunnel through to some other side?

I climb into the old wire-frame bed and lie on top of the stale linens. I type that I'm both sorry and okay, which provokes more calls. Christ, I should answer him. Explain it all, open my heart, make it plain, et cetera. But I can't. I can't speak. The words catch in my throat. Everything I can think to say is not only inadequate but false. Or will be made false. Is it the speaker or the listener who does the twisting, the distorting, the reducing? Is it me or Ellis who will draw a conclusion that I don't necessarily mean but also can't dispute?

I just can't think straight, I write. I promise to call him the next morning, and my phone darkens. Outside, a partial moon climbs the sky.

23

It's just shy of seven when I head down to the kitchen the next morning. Jiajia is already awake. She says good morning, then returns to tapping peaceably at her phone. The living room has been cleared of last night's clutter. The couch cushions have been fluffed and squared.

I'm not very familiar with the arrangement of items in my mother's kitchen, but I do my best to pretend. I rummage through the refrigerator for something to drink. I open each cabinet from one end of the kitchen to the other and pull eggs, oil, salt, an assortment of spices. Jiajia takes no interest in what I am doing.

I offer to make her some breakfast, but upon surveying the ingredients I've collected, she declines. While she remains absorbed in her phone, I crack the eggs and watch them flutter at the edges. A spider climbs the length of a dish towel hanging over the kitchen faucet.

"Why didn't you call me? Tell me he was here?"

"Ah, your father." She grins, as if sheepish on his behalf. "He didn't want to announce his arrival. He said, 'Who am I? The emperor?'"

"Ha. Right." With a spatula, I push the flat of eggs onto a plate. They're too wet, and somehow the fact that I produced the whole thing makes it even more revolting to me. "And what are your plans?" I ask. "What are you still doing here?"

"Wo, ah?" The early sunlight casts a faint blue glow across Jiajia's head. "Your father needs someone to take care of him. Too late in life for him to learn how to cook or clean. He doesn't even know how to use the laundry detergent."

So she's his maid?

"Not exactly," Jiajia demurs.

Does he pay her at least?

"It's not always about money, ba?" she says pointedly.

I carry my plate to the kitchen table, but Jiajia follows me, phone in tow. If he doesn't pay her, I press, she would be considered a slave. Does she see that?

"Close!" Jiajia purses her lips as if to bite back a smile. "I'm his wife."

There must be a strange expression on my face, because she moves toward me and puts a cold hand on my arm. "Ah! It's for my green card only. A paper wife and husband! It isn't real." Her cheeks redden as she keeps talking. "Sister, it's a very good thing for me. A blessing. I'm lucky your father came. Without your mom, I would have no one in this country. And no papers, you remember. I can't make it on my own. I've had to face this fact of my life."

"So. You're a—"

"Ai," she swats. "What will you call me now? Your words. Your horrible words. Try to understand me, Sister. Where I'm coming from."

"Sister" troubles me. My horrible words? What about hers? How does she use hers so brazenly? She calls me sister. Does that mean she calls him father? I would hardly even call him that. Did she call my mother hers, too?

Calm down, I tell myself. For a person largely estranged from my family, I feel oddly possessive of the monikers attached to them. My untouched eggs have grown cold, and that splotch of red ketchup brings bile to my throat.

"You're okay, ba?" Jiajia's brow is knit with concern.

"Fine. I'm fine." I push the plate a little farther away from me. For a while, we let the TV suck up the attention in the room. Jiajia sighs when the news pans a crowd of solemn faces on the shore. "These poor ah-migos. Don't they know? America is full."

Further reporting reveals it to be the eastern islands of Greece.

Jiajia nods her head. "Yes. Everywhere is full."

Eventually, my father pads down the stairs. He's wearing a slim, olive-colored coat, and for a moment, he's surprised to see me here.

"Zao." He nods at me. A cold greeting compared to yesterday's.

Jiajia places her phone on the wide leather arm of the couch and heads to the kitchen. She rummages through the refrigerator shelves. I hear glass or ceramic being placed gingerly on granite. The top of a saucepan rolls and settles. A spatula or wooden spoon hits the edge of a bowl as she stirs.

"Make some coffee. I'm so tired today," my dad says as he eyes my plate of uneaten eggs. "Would you like some coffee, too, child? You have a long drive home, do you not?"

.   .   .

After breakfast, my father belches quietly, then stands and tops his head with a thin-brimmed hat. He's headed to the garage, but I stop him. "Where's the piano?" I blurt before he can dash out the door. "Mom's piano."

"Ma-ma's pi-ano," he says, as if deep in thought. We look to the four pits in the carpet of the living room where our baby grand, that mahogany beast, once stood. It was a gift to her from him. I still remember the day it arrived at our house in parts. The fury with which she watched over the men who assembled the thing and righted it on its stout legs. She called him a bastard and a fool that evening. A man with no damn sense. While Mom shouted, Narisa tinkled the upper keys, which only highlighted the fact that no one knew what to do with the thing.

We were both tasked with lessons that year. I played diligently but without feeling. Surprise. Narisa played beautifully, our teacher said, but only on the rare occasion that she deigned to practice. Neither of us kept at it, and soon the house was deprived of what little music we'd brought to it. The piano eventually served as a triage for mail and newspapers.

"Mama's piano. Ha!" My father shakes his head. "She hated that thing," he says with a smile.

It was true she hated it. Not even Dad's nebulous talk of its investment value could assuage her. But she'd kept it all those years. And every afternoon she'd shut the blinds in the room where it stood to protect the piano's glossy wood from direct sunlight. She'd planned to bequeath it to me after she was gone. *Bequeath*. That was the word she used, in English. Perhaps she knew I wouldn't understand its Chinese rival.

"She said she would gift it to me. Before she died."

My father shrugs. "She was a giving woman. Always giving away what she didn't have."

"You sold it, I guess?"

Behind us, Jiajia rummages through the refrigerator shelves with great care.

"Ai, did you expect the house to remain a shrine to her memory?"

I suppose I did. What else did I imagine would happen to these belongings, to the house in its entirety, after she died?

Perhaps I thought if I left it alone long enough, it would all crumble to powder or sublimate into thin air.

Mom left no will or final word about her belongings, which I interpreted, maybe wishfully, as tacit permission to do nothing about them. Now I understand that perhaps there was no will, because there were no belongings. None of these things—the piano, the car, the house—were hers. Perhaps she'd always known that my father would come back to reclaim them.

"Objects are not memories, hai zi," my father says. I catch the faintest curl of his lip. "Only memories are memories. You understand."

I don't reply or even move, really. Does he really think he can offer me vague fatherly axioms after all these years? Dad looks at himself cockeyed in the mirror, a moment of vanity I had never seen in him as a child.

"I hear you are married," he says to his own reflection. "My good girl."

"I hear the same about you."

His lips part into a smile and he slips both hands into both pockets. "Ai, she's all grown up." He shakes his head. "My good daughter. Married." He pulls up a black, bifold wallet, opens it, finds it empty, then puts it away again. "I'll have a gift for you later." And he cannot resist adding, "A real one."

He slips through the garage door, and I hear Narisa's old car grumble to life. From the warped bay window, I see him speed down our street, turn the corner onto Beverly Road. The brim of his hat tilts left as he makes a right.

Ellis calls, but I can't answer him. I put my phone in the drawer of an old console table by the door. Outside, an early breeze nips at my arms. Dew from the grass wets my bare ankles as I make my way toward the car.

A Stone, a Statue, an Egg

Narisa did not return to her parents' house often. She spent her days at the warehouse, and afterward, she was with Gabriel. What did they do? Eat, mainly. Or ride their bikes along the canal until it met the Raritan and throw paper clips, deli clock-in receipts, gum wrappers, whatever was in their pockets into that swift green water. They experimented with various new sex acts, which were exciting if mutually dissatisfying to both parties (neither had had sex before, though Gabriel had a close encounter during his junior prom a year earlier).

What was it about her? Something about the way she spoke, the way she looked at people on the street like she might run up and bite them. She seemed constantly tense, vibrating with an energy that frightened and attracted him. It made him want to smooth her over, and he was not mature enough to understand that he was utterly unequipped to do this. He felt as if he were the owner of a large, dangerous dog.

In May, Gabriel's brother returned from college for the summer, which pushed the two lovers to spend their evenings together in Narisa's room at the warehouse. There was not much ventilation on the second floor. They sweated and turned through the night on the narrow, metal cot, which Narisa had moved closer to the window so they might catch the breeze that played down Casequake Avenue.

Gabriel brought his school laptop to her room, and they watched music videos or pirated network shows. They had weed-addled conversations about high school conformity and the hypocrisy of college applications. They theorized about Tupac's disappearance, about the presence of God. Gabriel was a year younger than Narisa and sometimes mined her for what she could remember of the answers to tests in physics and world history. Narisa obliged. They talked more and more about getting married. (This being such a distant reality to Gabriel that it felt safe to him. Like talking about a dream.)

On balmier nights, the kids climbed up the ladder, past the shelter and onto the roof, shared a joint or a beer. They sat on rusted folding chairs. Here was where Narisa revealed her plans to escape, and where she proposed that Gabriel go with her.

"We'll need enough for food, rent, and gas for your car," Narisa said. She calculated and recalculated the combined wages they earned between Gabriel's parents' deli and Narisa's father's warehouse.

"Gas to go where?" Gabriel prodded.

Narisa didn't have the answer to this. Or, at least, not a consistent one. She preferred to immerse herself in more logistical concerns. They made it feel like she was making actual progress: How much cash would they need in order to live on their own? Which NJ Transit buses went where? If the police were prevailed upon to search for them, for how long could Narisa and Gabriel reasonably evade them? Her thinking was frantic, circular.

Gabriel played along, suppressing the fact that his mother had enrolled him in an SAT prep course for the summer. He pored over transit maps with her, made plans to ditch the cell phone his mother had bought for him. Part of the pleasure in loving Narisa was that she could make any fantasy seem tangible. Things were always on the brink of becoming real, and the brink was an intoxicating place to be. He did want to go away with her, but that was the extent of his desire. Away, and with Narisa. Meanwhile there seemed to be parameters Narisa had in mind that she would not reveal.

He made the mistake of making his own suggestion once; he had a cousin who lived in Holmdel. They might stay in her extra room for a few months to test what living on their own was like.

"What's the point?" Narisa plucked at the nubby fabric of the blanket she had pulled from her bed at home. "Aren't we doing that now?"

Their legs were tangled together. Gabriel would remember that time as having been lived in bed. They were most capable of anything when their bodies were still and supine.

"I don't know." He toyed with the ripped belt loop on her jeans. "It's just a first step."

"Toward what?" She was surprised and disappointed by the smallness of his thinking.

"I don't know. Just an idea."

An orange cat slid past on the narrow window ledge.

Narisa would not sleep that night. She never did when Gabriel stayed over. Though she closed her eyes and lay motionless, something in her remained rigid and alert. Her mind wandered aimlessly, combing through memories, the events of the evening, the faces of her old friends, bits and pieces of their conversations. She tried feebly to convince herself that this stillness was sleep or just like it.

At six o'clock, Gabriel's watch alarm chimed, and he rose from their bed, silently gathered his belongings and got ready for school. After he left, Narisa fell into a deep, dreamless sleep.

• • •

Her birthday that year was a Sunday. June 7. And, at her father's insistence, Narisa made a rare appearance at the house. For her good—or, at least, uneventful—behavior, Jing gifted Narisa a car. It was a midnight-blue Toyota sedan from one of the used-car lots on the strip at Seven's Crossroads.

Sleek and long-bodied with cracked black leather seats. The girls both squealed at the sight of it, ran barefoot to the driveway where Jing had parked. They opened and closed the windows, the trunk. They tuned up and down the FM channels. They made a song out of the chirps that came from locking and unlocking the car doors.

Rita watched from inside as her husband herded the girls into the car for a test drive. From the kitchen, she could see him putting on a show. He pulled the seat belt into place, adjusted the rearview mirror. He calibrated his seat, checked both sideview mirrors. He put the car in reverse, gassed it down the long driveway. Narisa and Eleanor wore open-mouthed smiles, like dogs panting for air. Jing three-pointed the car, and they were gone.

That night they celebrated. Rita panfried two plate-sized pompanos for dinner and steamed a platter of egg and minced pork. Jing poured a can of beer into two glasses, one for himself and one for Rita. The girls shared a red Gatorade.

Though it was not her birthday, Jing had a gift for Eleanor, too. Since the Invention Convention, Eleanor had received all manner of advertisements and mailings from partners and sponsors of the Invention Convention—STEM-oriented charter schools, academic summer programs, college prep courses. It was a sort of routine for Jing to flip casually through them. "See? Even these people know to look for Eleanor," Jing would announce over a stack of letters and postcard ads each evening. "Our scholar has their attention."

After the excitement surrounding the car had settled, Jing held up a thick yellow packet that evening. "Girls in Science," it read. "Sponsored by Chevron."

Eleanor tore the envelope open. Inside was a brochure that featured diligent, confident girls with furrowed brows, engaged in stern, tentative conversation. Girls hunched over robotic Lego sets, and more girls wearing safety goggles, watching smoke rise out of a glass cylinder. Inserted between the last two pages of the brochure was a letter typed on grainy white paper, congratulating Eleanor on the acceptance of her application and welcoming her to the Girls in Science Program, a four-week camp based out of Fordham University for girls ages fourteen to seventeen interested in engineering and chemical sciences.

"Wah, Liu Jing, you're rich," Rita said without smiling. She turned her yellow rubber gloves inside out as she pulled them from her arms, laid them on the edge of the sink. "How did you find the money for such lavish gifts?"

"Find?" Jing gave her a laugh, then turned his attention back to his plate. "You mean earn."

Eleanor looked at the glossy folder. She didn't understand exactly. She hadn't applied for this program.

"Ah, application." Jing dismissed the thought. "You write your name and birthday. You pay a fee. Even this old man could achieve it." He winked. "A smart girl," he said, "needs to be challenged. Everybody knows. She needs to learn from smarter girls so that she knows what she's up against."

Rita snorted, slicked a cigarette from its box and opened the door to the patio. "And what do the dumb girls do?"

"They drive their new cars to work," Jing said. "They work hard and make themselves useful any way they can." He held an open palm to Rita, and she placed a cigarette in it. "Do you see? One daughter reminds us of where we come from; the other foretells where we will go."

Eleanor tried to get out of going to the Girls in Science camp. Scholarly interest was not a pose she had planned to hold for very long. She went so far as to approach her father.

Jing was packing for his annual trip to Taiwan. Linen shirts, light, breezy pants, a paper-thin jacket for rain. They all fit neatly into the massive suitcase, which yawned open like a mouth. The bulk of his suitcase was taken up by gifts for nieces and nephews, aunties and friends who had survived his mother, old classmates, business associates. Ralph Lauren sweatshirts, boxes of Almond Roca candies, bags of ground Dunkin' Donuts coffee, some English spelling books for children.

Eleanor helped her father fold his clothes and arrange his suitcase the way he liked it. Shirts and pants neatly folded, a field of socks in the bottom left corner, paired shoes bagged in clear plastic and lined up along one side. A Tetris of his belongings and objects that would soon belong to other people. Eleanor read the gifts like tea leaves, divining what the other half of their family might be like. The sidewalk chalk, jigsaw puzzles, and Disney tapes, for instance, alerted her to the fact that there were children in the family that they had never met.

Jing slipped a tube of toothpaste into a zippered pocket. "Your sister makes the same mistakes over and over again," he said. He looked up at Eleanor from where he knelt by his suitcase. "I'm a father, okay? When you have a child like that, you have to do something. You can't just sit back and watch. Like you're some kind of prince. Like you're God. Like there are so many disposable people around you."

Eleanor nodded.

"You see what I mean. I only have two of you." He tilted his head at a box of chocolates which sat at an angle on two uneven stacks of clothing. "You know the mistake women make? When they're ahead? When they're doing well? They always turn around. They look behind. They always reach backward to the slower and dumber ones. The ones who didn't listen.

"This is wrong, you understand. This is very bad, and you must learn it now. From me. I'm the only one who can teach you this. If you're ahead, you must not look back. Your sister must move forward to meet you. You are not to move backward. I would say the same thing to her if things were in reverse. Do you understand me?"

Eleanor said nothing. She stood still and straight. She unfocused her eyes so that she would not even blink. She thought of a tree, a stone, a statue, an egg. Somewhere in the world, girls were brave. They were drawn swords, raised fists, lone ships in the swell. But not here. Here, stillness was the weapon of choice. Dispassion a battle tactic. Here in her father's house, it was best to look somewhat dead in the eyes.

Jing stopped his packing and looked at her strangely.

"You must understand, Daughter." He moved toward Eleanor and wrapped his arms around her, gripped her in a tight hug. "We've always understood each other, haven't we? You and I," Jing said. A shirt button pressed into the skin of her brow. He was leaving them. That much Eleanor understood. He was leaving them, and he would not return.

The ceiling fan whirred above them and played tricks with the light in the room. Eventually, Jing's arms loosened and fell away. He put a hand on Eleanor's head. "You'll help your mother, ba?"

24

The warehouse is a squat, stuccoed building that sits like a church at the crest of a low hill. The patch of grass beside it is shaded by a row of tall oak trees shrouded with kudzu, where Narisa and I played as children, and where a small, uncollared dog sniffs about, urinates.

Inside, the walls are the same mustard color they always were. The distinct smell of mildewed cardboard transports me to the adolescent afternoons I spent here. The whole space feels much larger than I remember, maybe because the walls are no longer lined with stock. All the steel shelving units stand bare. And where it used to bustle with assemblage and activity and collaborative shouts, now the warehouse echoes with the sound of a few people chatting as they rip and flatten cardboard boxes at an unhurried pace.

A woman stands near them, wrapping a yellow cable around her elbow. I recognize her, I think. She always gave me and Narisa nasty looks, but I can't remember her name. She gapes as I walk toward her, and it becomes impossible not to stop and acknowledge her stare.

"This is Narisa?" she says and sets the cable down.

I correct her, but she remains happy to see me. And I admit it feels good to see her, too. A familiar face, any familiar face.

"How tall you are now!" she remarks. "And your face. So thin. You've aged." She makes a show of scrutinizing my facial features, touches the rim of her glasses and squints.

"You have a lady's nose now. Narrower. You used to look like a baby pig," she says. "Remember?"

I don't remember that, no.

To my left, framed by a small porthole in the office door, I catch my father's face watching us. I raise a hand at him, but he disappears out of view.

Before the woman can say more, I slip away and head toward the office. My father's lips tighten into two wan lines when I enter. He's surrounded by white bankers' boxes, filling them with unused office supplies, old stock, worn samples.

"You're chasing me," he says.

"You ran," I reply.

He coughs up a laugh and returns to what he's doing. Elastic hair bows spill out of opened bags as he tosses them into a box. A stack of binders on his desk threatens to topple over. Its landing would be softened by an impossible tangle of blue and pink clip-on hair extensions. A box at my feet is filled to capacity with unused pads of sticky notes. "This is it, huh?" I toe the box. "The end."

"Made in Taiwan." He enunciates the phrase in English, then examines a wooden comb carved with flat peaches and curling leaves. Into the box it goes. "Ai, it's all in the past now. Exporting this kind of junk, cheap stuff. It's a temporary business. No country can do it forever. Not if they're doing it right."

"What are you going to do, then? Stay here?"

His nostrils flare almost imperceptibly. I remember the tic from childhood, and seeing it again after all these years is not unpleasurable. "Why not? Perhaps I'll stay a little while."

"What about your family?" My cheeks redden at the thought of his wife and son in Taiwan. I was never jealous of those people. Or, at least, I'd convinced myself I wasn't. My stance was pity. I pitied them for entering any sort of covenant with my father. A man without allegiances. A coward.

"My family has gotten all they need from me," he says.

Somehow, I doubt that, but I don't have it in me to press further. Outside, that woman's voice carries toward us, punctuated by barks of her laughter and the low murmur of someone else's voice. "What's with her?" I ask.

He palms a pack of dog toys with desultory interest. "Women don't handle change well," he says without irony. "Now what do you want from me, hai zi?" He drags on the word "want" with some distaste.

I relay what I've learned from Jiajia. That the two of them are married. Or soon will be? My voice wavers as I elaborate. I feel like a schoolgirl tattling on a classmate.

"Marry! How will she marry anyone? The little fool. She's living in a dream world."

I give him a blank look.

"We're not married. She can't. She knows this. The girl has no papers."

"Isn't that the whole point of marrying you?"

"She would have to return to her home country to get this green card."

"Okay? So?"

"Yaa. Do you think they just hold on to your citizenship for you like a napkin you left at the dinner table? No. Deserters do not get to keep their place. Ship jumpers cannot simply return aboard."

Can you believe this: His eyes water as he speaks. His tongue gets caught and braces against the back of his teeth. Does he actually see himself in her predicament?

"She doesn't have a home country anymore. Not here, not there. No nation. She's a ghost. She doesn't exist. Therefore, I take care of her."

"Is that what we're calling it?"

He glares at me after that. "Ai, what do my children know about taking care? Who took care of your mother while you were gone? Your poor mother. Do you kid yourself and say it was you?"

I stammer a bit here—perhaps because I have kidded myself about that.

My father waves an awkward hand. "Okay, okay. Hao le," he says. "I'm sorry I brought it up. The past. It's my fault. Not yours. How can a child be at fault?"

From one of the boxes, he unearths a pack of off-color tissues and hands it to me. A gentle smirk, the kind you might pay to a baby or a dog for its naivete, appears on his face. "Go home and keep cleaning up her things, like you said. Memories will do you good. You can keep the girl company, can't you? We can give her that much. She talks about you often. And she's always wearing your old things."

.   .   .

Back outside the office, the woman considers me for a moment—my pink-rimmed eyes and splotchy nose. Without warning, she comes in for a hug. I feel the divot of flesh at her bra strap.

"Oh, little beauty. How long has it been since you stepped foot in this dirty warehouse?" she asks. "Ten years? Ah, it must be hard to see. So many years of work and sacrifice. Now all empty. Only the shell remains. Do you remember me? Do you even recognize me?" She stands back, as if to quiz me on my memory of her body.

I open my mouth with optimism, but no name comes out. Looking at her in that deep purple dress, I am reminded of an eggplant.

She chuckles. "Minru. I am Minru. Ah, why should you remember? You were never here. Narisa would remember me. Minru, Minru. I was the most loyal worker of them all." Here, she performs a little curtsy.

"Everyone has abandoned this place but me. Narisa stole off in the night. You went away to school. Peng, that poor man. Even his little girl made it out of here. Though not far. Only I stayed. I! For years and years. Nothing but silence. No one but strangers." She gestured at the three people working at the boxes. If they know they're being talked about, they don't let on.

"But you all come crawling back eventually, don't you? Ha! Even your father, the very owner of the business, tried to climb up and get away. And here he is again, is he not? They always return."

She moves closer to me but doesn't lower her voice. "The secret is that I'm not so loyal at all. I just know myself. I know where I ought to be. Do you, child?"

I smile politely at her but begin taking shallower breaths. Suddenly, I don't want to breathe her air, the moisture from her mouth.

"You see"—she raises a finger—"people don't know themselves. They have fantasies about who they are. All kinds of desire and ambition. That's how they get into trouble. Trouble and tragedy! It's because people don't see where they end and fantasy begins."

I bob my head as I back away and exit the way I came in.

Life Where?

Peng had been shy about complaining to Jing, but he was at his wit's end. Narisa and her boyfriend had gotten out of control. The thick stench of marijuana, the nightly grunts and moans and performative squeaks. And worst of all the laughter. Who had taught that girl how to laugh? They were not coy giggles or sweet, romantic murmurings, but horrific cackles that carried from her room to theirs.

Every night Peng and his daughter were subjected to such vulgar sounds. Was it that she wanted Peng to hear her? It was disgusting. And his poor daughter. How could he subject her to something so vile as this Narisa, who at first had appeared so good and admirable?

When Jing's brother Ah Mao arrived to manage the warehouse while Jing was away for the summer, Peng took the opportunity to broach the subject. "It's a delicate situation," Peng said to Ah Mao. "But I feel it's my responsibility to say something. She's up all night with her boyfriend," Peng said. "She drinks and she smokes."

And it was not just the nightly noise, Peng said to Ah Mao. In the mornings, Narisa appeared to work sometimes as late as eleven o'clock. (Ah Mao would not have known this, so rarely did he himself appear at the warehouse before noon.) She plunked down the narrow stairs in her slippers and shorts and disappeared into the office, emerging only to ask Minru how long it would be until this or that order was completed. Then, she would drive off to pick up a coffee or breakfast from the deli down the street.

Ah Mao was shaking his head before Peng had even finished his complaint. "Buddy, I'm just here to make sure you all don't slack off or revolt. Take it up with Jing when he returns, ba. I'm not the girl's father," he said, "and neither are you."

Minru gave Peng a knowing smile when he returned to his seat beside her. "A rich girl will only work for so long before she realizes she doesn't have to," she said.

Peng growled in agreement, though he didn't return the smug smile. He felt a sudden, inexplicable rage at Minru, at the crooked shape of her mouth, the curve of her back beneath her thin, clinging T-shirt as she bent over her yellow beading and black leather fringes. Was this hatred? Did he hate her?

"You smile?" he said lowly. "What pleasure does my suffering bring you?"

"Ai, Peng. Of course, I get no joy out of saying I told you so. I just knew. As a woman knows. This Narisa couldn't teach your Jiajia anything."

"You would speak this way about my family? About my brother's children?"

Minru laughed. A high bark. "What family treats its oldest brother like this?"

"In their eyes," she said, "you are just like the rest of us. Cheap labor. An absconder and a law breaker. Relation or not."

To Peng's chagrin, Gabriel returned to the warehouse that very night. Shortly after they'd arrived at the warehouse in January, Peng had gone so far as to approach Narisa. He had begged her to be a friend to Jiajia, to talk to her in English. To tell her anything—about American food, American nature, about school, about people. What a fool he'd been. Tricked by Narisa's long swan neck. Her serious arched eyebrows. Tricked into thinking that she was a fine, respectable woman.

Tonight, it all began again. The fighting, the banging, the squealing. Did Peng hear crying? How could he sleep like this? Peng lay in his cot, across the way from his daughter, down the hall from his niece, filled with the most repugnant desire, desire he tried to suffocate but that only hung in the room, on his skin like vapor. It was not just lust, though that was how it felt. It was also jealousy. He envied their youth. Their narrow, sexed bodies, their careening minds. He had been like that once, hadn't he?

What was left of him now but hands that worked? Shoulders that ached? Eyes that squinted at beads and fringes under bright lamplight? Oh, he was grateful, grateful, grateful, of course. Yes, grateful to America, to Jing, and to God. But also: He was tired of having to feel or feign gratitude. Of having to swallow his bitterness, like returning vomit and bile back into his body.

Peng crept out of the room and sat on the narrow, plastic bench in the bathroom down the hall. It also shared a thin wall with the girl and her boyfriend, but it was better than lying next to his daughter with an erection. There he could at least look down at himself. It took a herculean effort not to think of Narisa, or his wife, or his daughter, or Minru. Not to think of any of the women who swirled about his life, his past, his present, as he slicked his bruise-colored head. It was difficult, but he succeeded. He had thought only of himself, slipping in and out of a kind of wet nothingness. A familiar, disembodied tunnel.

. . .

In the muggy, late summer heat, the warehouse gave off an acrid smell of equal parts bleach and mildew. White sunlight fell through the windows (positioned too tall to reveal anything but the sky and the uppermost leaves of the nearby oaks). Eleanor had headed off to her summer camp in July, and Gabriel had started his evening SAT classes at the high school. Narisa found Jiajia sitting alone in a spot of sunlight on the warehouse floor. Her greasy, stick-straight hair shone in the sunlight. It fell in front of her face like a black curtain.

"You can read?" Narisa asked the girl.

Jiajia looked up at her, showed her teeth and grayish-pink gums. A book with a thick cardboard cover lay in front of her. It had once been Narisa's, a story about the different letters of the alphabet, forming a family, then a neighborhood, then a community, then a nation.

"Read to me," Narisa said. She was bored, and something had made her feel that she did not have to be. Was it the car that had done it? Or her newfound sex life? She was older now, and somehow, more powerful.

Jiajia did not change her smile.

"Or, I know. Say something." Narisa knelt beside her. "Anything, sister."

Jiajia shook her head and returned to her book. She flipped a page.

"Come on." Narisa's voice took on a high whine. She surveyed the table nearby. "Say 'wig.'" She pointed to a sample propped crookedly on a Styrofoam head. Someone had drawn eyes and a mouth on its face. "That's a wig. Woo-ig." She stood now and walked over to it, repeating the word a few more times.

"I'll give you a bag of chips if you can say it," Narisa wheedled. "You can do it. You have to." Jiajia looked to the table where Ah Mao normally sat, but he had gone outside for a smoke with Minru. "I'll give you a hundred dollars. You don't think I can? I'll show you. Come."

Jiajia stood. Narisa grabbed her hand, and Jiajia looked back at her book, bending her knees. "Leave it. No one will take it. Come on." She pulled the girl into the office.

There was a small black safe underneath the desk, which Narisa opened by dialing her own birthday. From inside, she pulled forth an unruly stack of puckered green bills. From the stack, five twenties.

"Just say one word. Any word." Narisa fanned the bills out for Jiajia. "You could have this." Jiajia stared at the money.

"Hello, hello, hello," Narisa said. Then she added in her mis-accented Chinese, "I know you could hear me. Say words."

They stood like this for a short moment, Narisa behind the desk and Jiajia in front of it. The five green bills between them.

Jiajia looked out the small window. The tree branches along the turnpike lolled back and forth. The leaves shivered all at once in all directions. It looked chaotic, she thought, but really they were blowing in a single direction: the direction of the wind.

"What is this?" Peng entered. He'd heard the nastiness in Narisa's voice from the warehouse floor. The strained menace. Had he heard her correctly? It had sounded like another girl. He'd thought a stranger had come in off the street.

"What are these tricks? Put the money away. Put it back right now," he said. He pointed to the safe a little desperately. Everyone knew where it was hidden, though they kept up the pretense of not knowing it was tucked behind the file cabinet beneath the water-warped file folders.

But Narisa didn't move, and Peng reached for the cash, put his hands over the bills as if he were covering something indecent. He wanted, maybe irrationally, to shield his daughter from it, as if he had found Narisa showing his daughter pornographic photos or Jing's underwear. "This is your father's. Do you understand?"

Narisa pantomimed a search for her father. "I don't see him," she said. "Not for months." She wanted someone to be abused in this situation. But who? Who was wronged here, and how could she point them out? "Why don't you take?" She nodded at the cash Peng was holding. "I won't tell nobody. I leave. You won't see me."

Peng stared at her.

She went on, "I know in one week you earn little from my father. Take it."

The palm of his hand made a hollow thud against her chest. Though he pushed her almost as lightly as he might push a door open, Narisa fell back in surprise. Her hip hit the edge of the file cabinet behind her, and she put an arm out for balance, knocking a box of acrylic headbands off the top.

Once she'd collected herself, Narisa left them in the office. She left the money on the table. The headbands, too. They were someone else's problem.

Upstairs, Peng would try to explain himself to Jiajia. He was wrong to hit Narisa, but a girl needed to learn how to speak to a man, he said. But this wasn't right, and he tacked another direction. He was being crushed, but he had nowhere to go. He had trapped himself (and Jiajia) here, and he was frightened. But this wasn't quite it, either.

"I don't know what will happen," he said. He heard Narisa's footsteps clang down the metal stairs. "We may have to run," he said. "We may have to leave this place." Every time he tried to explain, his daughter looked at him with neither sympathy nor disdain. Without any affect at all. Her face placid as the moon. It was the first time it occurred to him that—despite all her sweetness and amenability, her gentle silence—his daughter frightened him.

.   .   .

Rita suffered after Narisa ran away. She lay in bed for several days, where she drew from a seemingly endless supply of menthol cigarettes and roasted peanuts. Eleanor assumed the responsibility of taking care of her mother. She left peanut butter sandwiches and glasses of water on her nightstand. She emptied the ashtray—in the shape and color of a bright head of cabbage—by her bed. After school, Eleanor checked the sink for crumbs. She counted the cigarette butts in the ashtray on the porch. Just enough evidence to prove that Rita still came out of her room, that she was still alive.

Eleanor bustled about like an imperious little maid. Some part of her took great pleasure in bringing food, water, tea, cigarettes from the kitchen up to her mother's bedroom. She cleared away the trash that piled up on her mother's night-stand while Rita ignored her, pretended to sleep.

Eleanor felt that her mother deserved this lowness and abandonment. She'd spent years accusing the girls of being soft, weak from lack of exertion. She'd railed against their American lives, which had raised in them these distinctly American deficiencies. Her daughters had been softened by lax schooling, disrespectful friends, the soporific television shows of the early afternoon.

"Strangers to the whole fish," she muttered to herself as she sliced the blue fins away from the body of a dulled perch. She left its brutish head. "They haven't the slightest idea what this is for," she said as she bagged purple lint from the dryer into the leg of a pair of stockings.

In short, Narisa and Eleanor were unconditioned to the realities of life.

"Life where?" Narisa had asked once, but it had only earned her a slap on the head.

In response to everything they did—errors in receipt arithmetic, missed doctor's appointments, bad grades, seasonal allergies, bouts of motion sickness, moments of clumsiness, people they let slip ahead of them in line, glossies of blonde women they earmarked in magazines—there was but one conclusion. American life had ruined her children.

Wasn't it her own fault, Rita sometimes thought? They were mutations of her own making, bastardized and diluted by life in the country in which she'd insisted they be born.

She had dreamt of an American life, but not of American children.

Were they a kind of punishment? A monkey's paw conclusion to what she'd prayed for every night in that low-ceilinged room at her mother's house in Taipei? Where in these girls could she find her own resilience? Her resourcefulness? Her work ethic? Her stoicism? What was the point of children if not some continuation of one's own qualities? "These are my daughters? These foreign girls?" she wondered aloud when her daughters did foreign things.

All of this made it difficult for Eleanor to pity her mother, someone who had so often distanced herself from her children. Though she did look small and pathetic in her bed, crying over a loss she herself had heralded. How could she be so surprised, Eleanor thought, so hurt when Narisa had suddenly cured herself of the Americanness her mother derided so much? When she'd finally done the one thing both their mother and father had done? Started a new life? Left what was behind?

"Are you okay?" Eleanor said finally.

"No."

"Do you think Narisa's okay? Should we call the police?"

"No. Let her go. She's the smartest one of us." In the shadowy room, the light of the muted TV cast glares and shadows on Rita's face. Eleanor sat beside her mother, who petted her arm until she fell asleep.

Rita vacillated wildly that year. Sometimes she accepted Narisa's disappearance with great aplomb. "She did what was right," she would say. "You know this, as I know it. In all the great histories, a woman's loyalty has never been rewarded. My daughter can take care of herself. I am free of worry."

Later, she would find a lurid piece of news on the internet. A girl Narisa's age, pregnant, had fallen in front of an oncoming train in New York. Rita cried at this. She leapt out of bed, brought her laptop to Eleanor's room, the power cord trailing behind her. "Who falls? My daughter, my daughter. She was pushed. She jumped."

. . .

Eleanor continued with life as normally as she could. In September, school started, and when people asked where her sister was, she replied that Narisa had gone to college after all. She was surprised to find that not a single student, teacher, or administrator questioned this or cared much at all. "Good for her," Ms. Paridou said. "Your turn now." She handed Eleanor a stack of college prep pamphlets to look at.

Eleanor grew taller. Her face narrowed. She became even more serious at school. News of her father began to trickle forth from Ah Mao, who now permanently managed the warehouse and the buyer's side of the business. Jing had returned to live permanently in Taipei. Eventually, he would remarry and have a son.

Narisa, on the other hand, never sent word. Not to her mother, not to Eleanor, not to Gabriel. So, Rita reasoned,

Narisa was living, at least. You had to be alive to preserve such a long, unregenerate silence. Eleanor could not reckon with that. Alive? How could Narisa live her restless, petulant life without them?

Occasionally the phone would ring and offer only static at the end of the line. Was it Narisa? Rita wondered. Calling to apologize? To ask for money?

What was Narisa doing now that she had unburdened herself of them all? Rita wanted desperately to know, but her imaginings were totally directionless, fueled by how little she knew about her daughter. Had Narisa hitched west? Gone to New York? Had she fallen prey to narcotics, violent men, evil women? Had she been adopted by a well-meaning couple? Would she finish high school? Find religion? An acting career? Love?

Eleanor distanced herself from these frantic fantasies of her mother's. She suppressed all curiosity, all longing and regret. She buried herself in her studies. She graduated high school and attended university, where she made and kept a secret vow to herself. She would not look for either of them—the abandoners. She would not talk or wonder about them. This wasn't retaliation, she felt, but respect paid to their final wishes. Why should she impede her father's final trajectory home? Why would she betray her sister's wish to disappear?

With Narisa, there was nothing Eleanor could envision but her sister's last moments in the warehouse—what she would come to consider as Narisa's last moments alive. She could piece that morning together with utmost clarity. That was a Narisa she knew, a Narisa she did not have to strain to imagine.

It was a chilly October morning, but Narisa, always impervious to cold, would not have worn a coat. She would have padded down the warehouse stairs in her socks. She wasn't wearing shoes, for neither Peng nor his daughter Jiajia reported having heard any noise that morning.

Except for her shoes, she would have been empty-handed. Everything Narisa owned remained in her room at the warehouse. Books, clothes, backpack, MP3 player, makeup, pocketbook. Even her bike sat in the crawlspace by the refrigerator. It would have been dark at that hour, and Narisa would have navigated carefully past half-filled order boxes by the office, past the worktables in disarray, behind the wall of drawers overflowing with bright ribbons, wires, fringes, and bands. She would have unbolted the warehouse doors and nudged them open.

Outside, dew blanched the grass, and the wetness of the air chilled and darkened her skin, tinging it a faint blue. Narisa stepped gingerly outside, and when the warehouse doors latched shut behind her, she vanished.

25

Back at home, I work at my mother's belongings. Though she didn't leave a will, she did send me one final email in the last week of her life. A simple, perfunctory list devoid of sentimentality. I read it once and filed it away.

From: Rita HW Liu <rita.liu21.68@hotmail.com>
Date: Sat, July 27, 2013, 9:02
Subject: Your help
To: <liueleanr@gmail.com>

Dear Daughter,

Pack up my belongings please. Clean up the garden. You may dig up and give away plants if you do not wish to water. Return extra herbs to Master Li and request refund for unused.

Some items in the letter were more difficult to interpret, and in typical fashion, I glossed over them. I'm always catching myself doing this. Convincing myself that there is no meaning in those meanings I find difficult to understand.

Now I read the hard ones again:

Take care of your father.

Did they keep in touch, I wonder? No mention of Narisa. Did she know my father would return but that Narisa never would?

Make the home yours, Little Ziqin. You were happiest here, though you never admit it.

Did she mean I was the happiest of our family of four? Or that I was happiest as a child and then increasingly unhappy after that? Did she mean I didn't admit it then? Or still cannot admit it now?

I do recall being quite content in this house, though I wouldn't have dared to admit to being happy when we all lived in it. So often our house was filled with injured, resentful silences. Had this made me happy?

Once, my father left a large yellow bruise on the side of Narisa's face. My mother shouted at him, but this only earned her a bruise, too, on the back of her head where it hit the wall. Then he turned to me. "Are you the only good thing in my life?" he asked before climbing up the stairs.

Could this have constituted happiness? For a while, I admit that it did. When a man hits both of his daughters, it tells you something about the man. If he hits one daughter and not the other, doesn't it tell you something about the daughters? I was the best thing in my father's life, and avoiding eye contact with my mother and Narisa when he alluded to this was one of the secret joys of my otherwise dull and unattended days.

At school, no one looked at me. Most adults—my parents, my teachers—sought order, and I furnished this with veritable ease. What was in me that blended so seamlessly into their need for quiet, for order, that they forgot I was there? This was what they wanted, and this was what I wanted, too. To move undetected like a dark creature beneath the surface of a placid sea. I wanted ever to be below. I thought it possible that I might never need to come up for air.

.   .   .

I pull my mother's clothing, shoes, scarves, hats from her closet and begin to fold and bag them. I keep one shirt for myself, a favorite of hers. A red oxford whose wayward collar has been stained a pale orange.

Outside, snow falls in bottom-heavy clumps. My father's shirts sit folded on top of the lacquered dresser, and a few of his trim jackets hang in the closet. I resist an urge to box them up and leave them on the curb.

When the clothes are done, I turn to the planters hanging by the window filled with long strands of moldering peacock moss. I water them. They look like shriveled heads of hair. In the bathroom, her lotions and toners and serums still line the counter like a row of tireless soldiers. I throw these away.

What else? I spread her most private possessions out onto the carpet of her bedroom. In forgotten shoeboxes, I find letters written in organized Chinese ideograms, and then letters written in painstaking English. I order them pointlessly by date written. In paper grocery bags, I unearth titles to old cars, the deed to the house, tax documents dating as far back as the 1990s, drawings, sketches, and other evidence that she had an abiding interest in art and illustration.

I sort through folders of photographs and negatives. Hundreds of off-center pictures of me, Narisa, and other neighborhood children vying for the camera's attention, and later, as teenagers evading it. Pictures of my father, of the boyfriend Tommer, of women getting in and out of cars in the grocery store lot, of Jiajia, of various point perspectives of the canal. I organize the undated photos by topic of focus. A stack for family, a stack for strangers, a thin stack of self-portraits, in which she made herself a stranger.

I find hand-drawn advertisements for a boba tea shop. Another flyer for Chinese-made, hand-wrapped dumplings. In a lone file folder, two unsuccessful attempts at a real estate license. Beneath that, partly completed workbooks, stiffened by water damage, on traditional reiki healing. Tendrils of another self.

This is the moment I am supposed to learn something, is it not? The moment my grief crests and finds relief?

In the afternoon, I stumble out of my mother's room like a disoriented beetle. I'm lightheaded, and the sunlight cuts sharply in from the western face of the house. I've spent the entire day in here. I startle Jiajia, who's in the hallway, holding a towel in one arm, a pile of clothes in the other. Warm, wet air from the bathroom fills the hall.

She eyes the shirt I'm wearing. "You found all her things in there?" Droplets from her wet hair bloom on the shoulder of her robe. "Your mother told me you wouldn't want her things after she died. But I said to her, parents don't know what their children will want." She slides past me and moves toward her room (formerly Narisa's), and I follow her.

"Did you know"—she speaks so carefully, as if she's lifting a long skirt and sidestepping puddles in the road—"your mama thought you loved money. And that because she had none, that you didn't love her. She was filled with bad, cruel thoughts. Only hurting herself." She let out a long sigh. "I told her it wasn't true, but she couldn't be convinced."

I stutter an objection. Why is she even telling me this?

She looks at me, surprised. "We shouldn't have illusions about people, especially not after they die." The plastic hangers rattle as she flips through her shirts and dresses, like leafing through a dull magazine. "Eh! What's the matter with you? Sit down. Here, on the bed."

I sort of stumble into the room and toward the bed, fitting my head between my knees. Jiajia rushes to my side and runs a light hand along my spine.

"What's happening? Did you eat anything today? Did you even have water? You were so quiet up here like a little mouse."

I tell her I'm fine, but her cold hands feel good against my neck and face.

"Pale white," she says gravely. "Let me read your mai. Give me your arm."

I stretch a docile arm toward her. Though I never put much faith in these readings, I have always appreciated the calm, cool fingertips pressed at the inside of my wrist. My breathing slows. We sit on her bed as she holds my arm. My mother vibrates between us like a plucked chord.

Jiajia moves her hand to my neck, where she seeks something (I don't know what) in the space just below my ears. A pale tongue emerges from her mouth, and briefly we stare at each other like this before I understand that she wants me to do the same. I open my mouth, and she inspects the surface of my tongue. Some part of me wants her to discern that I'm pregnant. For an impartial bystander to see it in my eyes, my skin, my tongue.

I stare at her, willing her to arrive at the answer.

"Stagnation," she diagnoses.

"I should have eaten." I nod as if in agreement.

She shakes her head. "Something ails you."

"This," I play, "is ailing me."

But she doesn't laugh. She gives me a sympathetic look, and I sit deflated on her bed.

. . .

Maybe it was true about the money. I wanted nothing from the house, from anyone, when I left for college, but I did accept the tuition money from my father that appeared as checks in the mail wrapped in slips of white paper. No notes.

Every semester, I wanted to rip them up, but, every time, I lacked the courage and financial solvency to do so. I couldn't bear to part with such a massive amount of money, and each semester I completed at school made it even more difficult to do so. This was the bond between me and my father. Unspoken, unconditional, utterly controlled by him. He did not really disappear that summer, not the way Narisa did.

It was when the first check arrived that I changed the narrative from culpable disappearance to tragic death. It was easier for me to swallow, to name and embody. The money was a reward for my suffering, a father's life and love cut too short, rather than what they likely actually were: balm for his feelings of guilt.

There was never a return address on the envelope, and I didn't dare ask my mother if she knew where he was. I submitted the tuition money directly to the bursar's office, and the relief when I did so each semester painted a pale wash over any stupid indignation I thought I deserved to feel.

My mother must have known about these monies but never directly asked about or discussed them. I suppose Jiajia knew about them, too. She seemed downright cozy with both of my parents. At the time, I wondered how we all hung together, so to speak. What strange, delicate thread tied us all to each other.

26

Every day, I tell myself I will go home, go to Ellis. I will pack up my things and leave the tangle of the house, Jiajia, and my father behind. But every day, I stay where I am. I work at my mother's belongings, which are not so innumerable, but which can be combed with greater attention, sorted into finer and more specific arrangements.

Each morning, my father and I exchange a terse goodbye as he leaves for the warehouse. Jiajia sends him off with a plastic container of lunch and an overenthusiastic wave of the hand, which he does not reciprocate. Then, she begins her household chores—mixing, pulling, frying, steaming, broiling, dusting, mopping, sweeping, wiping. She works unhurriedly, humming along to whatever plays through her earbuds, or setting up certain jobs (folding, ironing) so that they face the television.

It occurs to me that I'm watching her. That every time I walk past her, I inspect her work without fail. What am I looking for? Negligence? Error? I scrutinize what she watches on TV. I try to recognize her music from its faint but audible bass line. I peer at the screen of her phone when it chirps. She doesn't seem to notice.

I'm watching her, but I'm not getting the information I want. And what I want to know is if she and my father have sex. How far do the fingers of this pretend marriage reach exactly? Who is getting what? Who is taking advantage of whom? From what I can tell, they seem to occupy two separate rooms—my father in his old room, Jiajia in Narisa's—but this only confounds me further. At night, I listen for movement—beds creaking, fabric rustling, moans escaping Jiajia's or my father's throat, etc. It's depraved and embarrassing to be doing this, of course. Listening for something means you're already hearing some version of it.

But the listening only produces other sounds. Jiajia's slippers scuttle the floor. The floorboards creak underneath her. My father types messages audibly into his phone, sends them whooshing to their recipient. The refrigerator door opens, the water in the kettle boils. One night, I am listening so intently that I can make out the rhythm of a spoon knocking against the side of a ceramic mug.

Late in the afternoon, I climb out of my bedroom window and ease onto the sloping roof above the kitchen. This is where I used to sit and watch the surface of the canal or eavesdrop on my parents' conversations on the deck below. Ellis answers the phone after a few rings.

"Eleanor," he says. "When do we get to the point in the conversation where it all comes out? You're still my wife, right?"

We use those possessives (my husband, my wife) so rarely with each other that the word makes me laugh in awkward surprise.

I'm not sure what to say. But saying nothing is not an option anymore—I know that. I can feel myself reaching Ellis's limits, the way you feel the air thicken as you approach the sea.

"I do love you." I pluck out the words. "I feel that merits saying right now."

"Jesus." A laugh escapes him. "Thanks, I guess."

"I just need some time to sort things through. Organize my life. Everything is muddled together. Nothing feels clear enough. Does that make sense? I can't see straight with everything touching everything else. Cross-contaminating."

"You sound . . ." Ellis ventures, then alters course. "Why don't I come to your mom's? I could stay with you."

I have to laugh at this. "That's the opposite of what I just said."

"But I could help you."

"Ellis: He always has the answer, and the answer is always him."

"Okay, twist it around any way you want," he says. "But actually, that's how it's supposed to be. You're supposed to be my answer, too. I mean, usually you are."

Sunlight bleeds out of the sky, and its gold light threads the thin ripples of the canal. I run my finger along a notch in one of the asphalt shingles where I once tried to carve out my name.

"I'm waiting, Len," he says. Is this love? Waiting, patience, forgiveness? It feels as if it's all a language I recognize but never learned to speak.

He's waiting. I'm waiting, too. But I can't locate the part in me that will satisfy us both, that can be spoken and will still be true. Where is it? What is this levy in me made of, and when will it break?

"I know you need space, and I want to give it to you, let you grieve. All of that. But at a certain point doesn't it feel like space just begets more space? You're so far away, Len. Irretrievable. You won't talk about your mom. You won't talk about Samir. You're pregnant, but this seems vaguely off-limits, too."

"Maybe it's normal for there to be parts of me that you can't touch," I say carefully.

"No. You're a chronic avoider. But some things have to be faced." He takes a quick breath. "Is the baby even mine?"

Blood burns in my face and neck. How badly I want her just to be mine. How repugnant and impossible to think that she could be anyone's at all. Still, I can feel my possessiveness of her possessing me. This cannot possibly be love, can it? This is more desperate, more craven. Frost glitters on the lawn below.

"Maybe she's no one's," I offer. I think this is clever, but Ellis doesn't seem to care.

"She." I can hear the smile in his voice: "It's a girl."

Where Are You?
What Are You Waiting For?

Jiajia was on the second floor of the warehouse when the officers arrived, and, hearing the tumult downstairs, she took off her shoes. Strange men shouted. A woman wept, but having never heard Shan or Minru cry before, Jiajia didn't know who it was.

She held her sneakers at the heels and walked in her socks to the storage closet. Downstairs, more shouts and cries. Jiajia worked quietly. She laid a tall, cardboard box on its side. She stacked a few empties on top, then crawled inside, pushing her way into a nest of dog costumes with their matching hats and slippers. Princess dogs, Spider-Man dogs, hotdog dogs. They smelled faintly of chlorine. The glitter scratched at her face and arms. She pulled the box flaps closed.

By pressing her ear to the floor of the box, she could make

out a stranger's voice below, calling out short phrases that went unanswered. Commands. Minru shrilled once but was silenced by the stranger's voice. Jiajia did not hear her father, but she knew he wasn't one to shout or cause a fuss.

Footsteps shuffled and retreated toward the double doors at the back entrance. There was the muffled slamming of car doors. Still, Jiajia waited. A man's heavy step climbed the stairs and moved from room to room. The floor creaked as he walked. Each door released its particular whine as it was thrust open. "Anyone left in here?" he called once. Jiajia held her breath.

Eventually, all was silent. Still, she did not move. From a crevice between the box panels, Jiajia watched the light in the room sink into a rheumy yellow, then dusk orange, then darkness. She fell asleep for some time, dreaming as she often did, of a small body of water reflecting a row of low, white houses, framed by wooden beams and lined by a dirt path, wide enough for pedestrians and motorbikes but nothing else. Nearby, pomelos dangled from trees, fat orbs bowing their branches. People plunged their clothes and towels in the water, rubbing and wringing them. Somewhere in her mind, she understood, she was dreaming of wintertime. She dreamt of home.

How does a dream work? Though her mother never appeared in these visions of her old home, Jiajia would wake up thinking she had seen her. Dreamt of great beauty and an angelic voice. (These were the qualities of her mother's that

Peng most insistently wanted Jiajia to remember.)

But Jiajia had been five years old when her mother died. Old enough that she could still distinctly recall, without the help of photographs or her father's reminders, every aspect of her mother's face. Her straight, squared eyebrows, the raised mole perfectly placed to look like a stud in her earlobe.

Were those angelic? Things of great beauty? Her father would say yes, of course. Her mother's beauty had been like a river trickling over uneven stones. And her voice, like the sun's first morning ray, peeking through the leaves of a maple tree. Flowery words with no meaning. Or, at least, meanings that seemed to sail past her. As if he were saying something only for himself to hear.

He was never so poetic at the warehouse. But when they took the 116 to the grocery store between the Korean spa and the Home Depot, he seemed to have so much to say. He came alive when he sat on that bus. Words tumbled out of him, and Jiajia watched him attentively as he spoke, even though he just gazed out onto the road, following the railing that lined the highway. She worried that he might turn to her and find that she was not looking at him.

"I have nothing that matters," he'd said earlier that week. He stared out at the green, rain-drenched landscape. "Nothing of value. No fine clothes, no good shoes. My teeth are falling out. My wife has gone. I have nothing for you."

Her mother, her mother. Jiajia wondered if she would have liked these flat American lands they were passing by—

so green and unpeopled.

"But I have you. My greatest treasure. My growing treasure. I'm taking good care of you. I cook hot soup for you. I make sure you eat enough meat. I teach you lessons. You might not even know sometimes when I'm teaching you. I'm a very good teacher."

Another passenger shushed him. (He was talking very clearly, as he always did. He never whispered. He never mumbled.)

"Ai, I have nothing else. I don't want anything else. I don't even have my life. My life is yours. Did you know that? Everything I do. My work, my money, they belong to you. Obvious, right?"

Jiajia leaned her head against him, letting the sharpness of his shoulder rattle against her temple.

"Ai, my daughter. You screamed so much as a baby. I didn't sleep for the first three years of your life."

The bus trembled as it picked up speed. The side of Jiajia's head bounced painfully on her father's shoulder, but she kept it where it was.

"Ai, child. I wondered earlier on if I shouldn't beat the words out of you. But I didn't have the courage. And anyway, I thought it might be for the best. We would move to America, and you could have a fresh start. Learn English with no accent, no memory tangling up your tongue."

She stared now at the back of the seat, looking for some pattern in the odd shapes of the upholstery. She couldn't find the motif, where it began and where it ended.

Her father touched her chin gently. "Where are you?" he asked weakly. "What are you waiting for?"

. . .

Rita had been sitting alone at her secretary desk when she received a call from a stranger.

"Mrs. Boss," a voice said. "I'm Victor Zhang. I work for you." Though his voice was ragged, he spoke clearly. The buzz of men's voices could be heard in the background. He explained the events of the previous day.

"Are you safe?" she asked. He said he was. His brother had posted his bail, and he would wait for summons from home.

"And the others?"

"They have to stay," he said, his voice curling around what he was about to say, "unless they make bail."

"And how much is that?"

He told her.

Rita balked. "Each?"

"Yes."

"Where would I get that kind of money?" she said. "Where is your employer? Where is Ah Mao?"

"I'll call him next."

"You didn't call him first? You think I'm so broken-hearted for you people? I'll run down to the police station with cash in hand for each of you? Forget it, ba."

"There's one more thing—"

She held her breath, pressed the phone closer to her ear. Wasn't that like her? Rita could never resist one more thing. One hanging thread, one last clue. What was it in her that reached out always to take some chance?

Victor said in the same careful, curling voice. "One of Peng's belongings remains in the warehouse." Then he hung up the phone.

. . .

No one came to look for her. She drifted in and out of sleep. Hours passed. The sun rose and fell. The moon, too. She was afraid to move. She thought someone would come back, which she both wanted and feared equally.

She remained folded. Her legs were tucked in toward her ribs, her arms close to her body. Like an acrobat, she thought. Like a magician's assistant. Like a baby bird inside its egg. She urinated several times. And based on these punctuation points, she guessed it had been two days. She decided: If her father came back to find her, she would live. If her father did not return, she would die.

On the third day, she heard someone call her name. A woman's voice.

"Jiajia," the voice said. "Come out, ba. It's all right." It was the boss's wife. Narisa's mother. Jiajia slid out of her hiding place, from the soiled costumes and playthings that had cushioned her. She slipped her feet into her shoes and tied them.

"There you are," Mrs. Boss said when she saw Jiajia appear at the top of the stairs. "Aiya, poor child," she said rather expressionlessly.

Jiajia wanted to cry. Her body ached. Urine stained all sides of her dress. But for some reason, Jiajia did not know why, she smiled. Then, for the first time in six years, she spoke. She said, with that daft smile on her face, "Hello, Mrs. Boss. Thank you for coming to find me. You're so generous. Do you know where my father is?"

Rita was not some charitable soul, some angel on God's mission to protect His creatures. "I am not some charitable soul," she told Jiajia as she held the girl's hand and walked her to the bathroom. "A young woman must find a way to rise on her own, no matter how difficult her circumstances."

"Yes," Jiajia said unsteadily.

In the shower, she bent to scrub her legs and feet. She said the word again to herself. Yes. Water trickled past her lips into her mouth. She had a beautiful voice, she thought.

. . .

When she heard the water shut off, Rita fed a towel through the space between the shower wall and its curtain. Jiajia pressed it to her face and chest. Luxurious towel! It was so thick, it could have made a sweater or a cozy comforter. (Though it stank of mildew from never having dried properly.)

Rita followed the girl to the bedroom she shared with her

father. "How old are you?" she asked.

Jiajia was twelve.

"Ah. I thought you were younger." Rita nodded at a box in the hallway. "I didn't know what you would need, but I brought a few things." She tugged the box by its flap into the bedroom and deposited all of her items in the closet that held Jiajia's and Peng's clothes and shoes. Aside from the towel, Rita had also brought some noodles, clothes that were much too small, a few pairs of socks tucked into each other, a pair of scissors, four chocolate bars. She was briefly startled to find Narisa's clothes hanging there, but she said nothing about this.

Rita picked up her shears and pointed them at Jiajia's head. "May I?"

Jiajia nodded and sat in a chair whose faux-leather seat was almost entirely peeled away.

"Your baba has been detained," she said.

Jiajia did not answer.

Rita forced a comb through the knots in the girl's hair. "It should be Ah Mao's responsibility, but of course he's nowhere to be found."

Rita knew herself to be skilled with the scissors. She cut large, confident swathes, just as she'd done when she cut fabric for the dresses she and her mother had sewn in Taiwan. She trimmed the girl's hair to what she thought was a stylish but practical length. Wet hair like blades of cut grass fell on Jiajia's shirt, her shoes, the floor. The girl started to cry. She knew even without a mirror: It was not a good haircut.

"He will be okay," Rita said. She touched the girl's shoulder. "I'll find Ah Mao. And I spoke to an officer there. He says the process is long but not unfair." Did Rita believe this or was she just saying it to soothe the girl?

"And if he's a good father, he'll say nothing about you. If they ask about you, he'll say you don't exist or that you died," she said. "We'll see what kind of man he turns out to be. Some men are incapable of putting their love aside." What about this? Did Rita believe this? "Women, too," she added for good measure.

After the botched haircut, Rita took a brief tour around the warehouse. It was empty. She'd thought some others would have been left behind or would have returned by now. She couldn't leave the girl here all alone.

"My family has left me. I'm all alone," Rita said as Jiajia pulled at the new ends of her hair. "I need someone at home with me. Will you come?"

They repacked Rita's items in the same cardboard box she'd brought them in. Jiajia collected her belongings in a plastic bag. A wooden hair comb in the Japanese style, a pilled peacoat (it had been Eleanor's), some shirts and underwear, her father's glasses, an envelope of cash and documents.

At home, Rita let Jiajia pick which room suited her. Eleanor's or Narisa's. Eleanor had already left for college without much fanfare. A stiff hug goodbye, a promise (which was not upheld) to visit during holidays. The truth was Rita did not know which daughter was more likely to return. Which had disappeared for good, and which was making a torturous, but ultimately circular, orbit. When Jiajia demurred from making the decision, Rita said brusquely, "You can have both, then," and moved onto the linen closet in search of clean sheets and blankets.

.   .   .

Peng had made a single phone call to the warehouse hoping his daughter would answer, but he was mostly relieved when she didn't. Perhaps, he hoped, she had just evaporated into thin air.

Victor was collected by his brother from the county jail within a few days. The women—Peng didn't know what happened to them. They had been separated from the men at the local precinct, and he never saw them again. There were rumors among the rest of the detainees that the women were being sent to a federal holding center in Massachusetts. But these rumors were propagated in English and Spanish, so Peng didn't hear them. Soon, everyone he knew was gone.

At every opportunity available to him, Peng called the warehouse, hoping and fearing for news of his daughter, praying that Ah Mao would pick up and lend him the money for his bail. But there was never an answer. Days passed. Some of the detainees were assigned to individual cells, and

others were relegated to firm blue mats on the floor of a large
room with many small windows. The large room smelled
foul, filled with men and their unwashed hair and bodies.
Still, Peng preferred the drafty room to the cells. At least in
the big room he could stare out of the window each morning
and watch as light touched the asphalt outside. And anyway,
he preferred to sleep close to the floor.

More days passed, then weeks. One morning, the men
were commanded to wait in line, and while they organized
themselves, it was revealed that one blanket and one pillow
would be distributed to each person. "Finally!" someone
shouted. There was laughter. A few men even broke out into
song. The prospect of a warmer night's sleep was comforting, though it did imply they might be there a while.

A young man approached Peng, who had spoken to no
one since Victor was let out.

"My girlfriend," the boy said, "es china."

Peng nodded at this but did not understand.

"Girl-friend," the boy said again. Then pointed to Peng.
"Like you. But prettier."

They played two rounds of chess. Peng won, and so did
the boy. Peng declined a third match, not wanting a tiebreaker
to reveal a clear winner and loser. The boy invited Peng to sit
with him and the other dark-skinned men at dinnertime, but
Peng said no. He ate his soft, chilled sandwich alone.

A few hours later, this same boy would find Peng hanging
from a low light fixture in the bathroom. The man's face was

blue, like a wet stone. A pilled blanket was twisted and rolled neatly around his neck. Peng's head was lowered, supplicant. It's possible that if the boy had seen Peng's empty, yellowed eyes, he would have caused more of a scene.

.   .   .

At home, Rita could not bring herself to explain to Jiajia where her father had gone. By the time she had finally called again to inquire about the status of his detainment, Peng had been dead for three days.

Her own words burned in her mind: We'll see what kind of man he turns out to be. Rita chastised herself. Why had she said this about a man she didn't know? About a man whose daughter would never see him again? What had she even meant by it? Cruelty was often meted out in empty, careless words like these.

Ah Mao, that old dog, reappeared eventually. He and Jing paid the fines for their illegal laborers, and the business picked up again as if nothing had happened. Minru, who in fact had her green card, cleared up her residency status and returned to work. She never saw the others again. Did they know about Peng? Why should she tell them? New workers arrived like the first buds of an inevitable spring. She didn't befriend them.

For some time, Minru was tormented by the mystery. Who, exactly, had reported Liu Enterprises as an employer of visa overstayers, border crossers, etc.? A neighborhood vigilante? Some principled citizen who worked in the space across the office park? Her mind twisted and turned down the varied avenues of possibility. It may have been Jing himself, who had not been returning Ah Mao's phone calls and likely wanted out. Or it could have been Rita, that spiteful woman, taking aim at her unfaithful husband. Or that bad daughter, who tramped about the warehouse, jaw set with antipathy and revulsion. Oh, there were too many possibilities, Minru often thought. This damn family. They made her head spin.

. . .

Rita enrolled Jiajia in the middle school. (Why hadn't this Peng enrolled her in school?) The girl learned quickly and did quite well for someone whose elementary school credentials Rita had invented. The woman felt some misplaced pride, as well as some confusion about Jiajia's scholastic success. Hadn't Jing mentioned that this girl was mute? Perhaps Jiajia had only been muted around Jing. Or even around her own father. So many men did not see their own domineering influence on others, she thought.

Over the years, Rita grew very fond of Jiajia. She would even come to love her, though she didn't dare ask or wonder if Jiajia loved her, too. It was easy for an old woman to love a young one, but not the other way around.

Rita tried to be happy, to seek small joys. Briefly she worked as a hostess at a Sicilian restaurant. She revisited her photography. She took a handful of French lessons at the community center where she met Tommer, a younger man who took her to dinner a few times a month. But seeking these joys exhausted Rita, actually. She felt she was too old to pretend.

In the third year of living with her, Jiajia was not surprised when Rita revealed that she was ill. Or, more precisely, she was unsurprised that the woman would need more taking care of. She did not love Rita, but she did feel some tenderness toward her.

In addition to performing household tasks and chores, Jiajia did her best to repay Rita's generosity by being generally companionable. She was understanding of Rita's dour moods, attentive to the increasing pallor of her skin. After some days of processing her diagnosis, Rita asked Jiajia to stay and take care of her. And Jiajia, having no real alternative and no living family that she knew of, obliged.

27

That night, I take Jiajia to the mall. I've been at my mother's house for nine days and am finally feeling the need to get out, stretch my legs. Plus, I want to buy something for Jiajia. It's undeniable to me that I owe her something, though the precise details of the debt remain unclear.

Maybe it's just the season of feeling indebted to others. The mall is busy with holiday shoppers. Its glass atrium is adorned with glittery holiday trimmings—green leaves, red bows, golden bells. Every storefront features some contractual incentive to buy. Buy one, get another. Spend here today, save here tomorrow.

Jiajia touches everything as we pass through the racks of department store clothes—every shirt, every dress. Jewel-toned fabrics and beaded objects, in particular, draw a reverent hand.

"Let me buy you that," I say about each piece she lingers on. "It's a gift, a thank-you for all your help with the house and my parents," I explain.

But she doesn't say anything, just shakes her head, which triggers a fluttering of her eyelids. I find myself annoyed. Doesn't it bother her to be wearing my old shirts? Narisa's dresses from high school? And why can she accept gifts and care from my parents but not from me? I leave her to her perusing and pick through the racks myself. From a rack by the cash register, I select a few sensible shirts, a pair of fleece-lined leggings, a knee-length, woolen skirt and buy them in a bit of a huff.

"These are for you." I hand her the large, paper bag. "Okay?"

"Okay." She nods and offers me a perfunctory thank you.

We eat dinner at the food court. Saucy noodles coiled in paper troughs. My mood improves as we eat, and I regret my brusqueness from earlier. I try again to be sisterly and warm.

I talk about my own problems as a way, I hope, of inviting her to talk about hers. She expresses no surprise in learning that I left my job at the lab. When I mention that Ellis and I are at a sort of impasse, she nods, gestures at my wrist where she had read my meridians.

"Disharmony, remember?" She toggles her eyebrows knowingly.

"Yes," I reply.

After that, we fall to silent chewing. We're seated by the trash bins, and people are continuously pausing by us, sorting their trash from their recyclables, stacking trays onto other trays.

I try to get Jiajia to drink. I buy two beers from the same stand where we ordered our meal. I even take a few sips from mine, in the hope that she might naturally follow my example. Am I loathsome? I want her to admit something, anything about her life. Why are the details of my life so diagnosable to her (disharmony) but the details of her life so obscure to me?

"I can't, Sister," she says when I press my plastic cup to hers. "Even your father doesn't know this yet, but you can know the truth." She serves me that broad smile, then pats her belly with her fingertips. "But don't tell him. It's still early. I'll wait a little longer before I say it."

.　.　.

On the drive home, the streetlights flare in my eyes. Sparse pines race past a backdrop of dusky yellow sky. Aren't coincidences supposed to be funny? The thought of us both being pregnant makes me depressed.

Who exactly is this Jiajia? The story was always that she and her father were our long-lost family, but we never treated them as such. My father employed Peng, his supposed brother, but did him no special, familial favors. That man never saw the inside of our home.

We gave Jiajia our old books, coats, and clothes, fresh presents on Christmas. Narisa got close to her, I think, while working at the warehouse. But I admit I treated Jiajia coldly on the rare occasion I saw her.

After Peng took his own life, my mother took the orphaned Jiajia in, but also put her to work as a housekeeper. It's the least we can do, my mother said when I objected to the arrangement. Was it the least we could do? Who was Jiajia to us, really? Was it duty or pity that yoked us to her and her to us? Was it ludicrous that no one would say, or ludicrous that I alone needed to know? Needed it to be one clear reason?

At a traffic light, the engine of Ellis's car shuts off automatically, and in the quiet I can hear Jiajia's nose whistling.

"Why are you still here?" I have to ask. "I'm just trying to understand. You don't owe anything to her. I just want you to know that. And definitely not to me. Or my father." The light casts its orange glow on Jiajia's face and neck.

"Or maybe you loved her," I pose. "And she loved you." The words sound so pleasant and simple. Like I'm reading a baby book, or directions for a recipe.

"Owe!" Jiajia says. "Why should I owe her anything? There's no sense in paying debts to the dead. Maybe I did love her."

The car rumbles as we drive down a section of asphalt that's been pulled up and not yet repaved. Jiajia's voice shakes. "I never thought of her as a mother. She never called me her daughter. But why not just call it love? If I saved love only for my own mother and father, where would I be?"

I ask if she really thinks my father will stay and take care of her. Perhaps it's a disingenuous or rhetorical question. But she takes her time to consider it.

"No one can stay forever," she says. "It's just as possible that I won't stay to take care of him."

I follow the street in silence. Roadwork on Canal Street takes us down a dark, winding detour—past the old water tower, past the abandoned trailer lot, past the spare cemetery where my mother received a Christian burial. (Her late religiosity was another surprise that bubbled up in the wake of her death.) At a curve in the road, a pair of animal eyes light up in the headlights and then disappear with the body they're bound to.

28

With Jiajia and my father's consent, I donate my mother's belongings to assorted organizations I've been contacting throughout the week. Extra blankets and bedding are welcomed at every shelter this time of year. Same with coats and winterwear. Books, CDs, and VHS tapes are accepted indiscriminately at a used bookstore in the center of town. At a nearby antique shop, I offload vases, trinkets, decorative jars, and boxes housed in larger decorative jars and boxes.

None of this is gratifying, and I feel silly for having thought that it would be. No one is interested in examining my mother's items or asking about their origins. Mostly, they point at a space on the floor where my boxes, meticulously labeled, can be stacked or pushed alongside other boxes and bags. The owner of the antique shop at least gives my items a perfunctory look-over before handing me a five-dollar bill from the register.

All the rest (old bottles of lotion, blocks of scented soap, pilled bras and underwear, childhood drawings and birthday cards, stuffed animals won at fairs and given as gifts, plated and tarnished jewelry, envelopes of dried flower petals) is garbage. Objects are not memories, I repeat as I lug bag after bag to the curb for collection. Though part of me knows that memories are not quite memories, either.

I store all of my mother's papers in several large accordion folders. One for official documents, one for her letters, and one for the photographs and film negatives she amassed over the years. These I stack on a shelf in the attic.

I keep two prints, which I slip into the pocket of the car's passenger door, lest I forget to take them home. One is an unsmiling portrait of her, a small square passport photo that must have been taken just before she emigrated to New York. The expression on her face is somber. Her chin is lowered, and her black hair billows around her face. There is a white, wormlike mark on her otherwise unblemished cheek. A speck of dust caught in the developing process.

The other photo is of me and Narisa. Years ago, our mother arrived unannounced at the elementary school asking for us. "Family emergency," she said solemnly to the school administrator when we appeared. She herded us out the school's front entrance.

She drove us to a treeless area near a dilapidated barn where the grass was dry and yellow and where she finally explained that she wanted to take our photographs during the rare solar eclipse happening that afternoon. There were special glasses you could buy to watch it through, she told us as she pulled and posed our arms, but she hadn't brought any. "Close your eyes," she said as she backed away with the camera to her face. "You'll go blind if you look."

There's nothing strange or even interesting about the lighting in the photo. Maybe it looks later in the afternoon than it actually was. Otherwise, there's no indication that a rare celestial event is taking place. It looks like any other sunny day. Nothing out of the ordinary is expressed by the two of us, either. Just two sisters standing with their eyes closed and their feet obscured by the uncut grass.

. . .

My father informs me of his plans to return to Taipei with no promise or indication as to when or if he will return. I don't care what he does. And perhaps it's due to this indifference that I am able to speak more directly with him. I wait for the right moment to confront him, after Jiajia leaves for one of her afternoons at the acupuncturist's office. When I find my father, he's in the kitchen cutting a papaya into wedges and cubes. His head is lowered in concentration, shoulders raised.

"Are you avoiding me?" I approach him from behind. "It's interesting that two weeks after I get here, you decide abruptly that it's time to go."

My father turns and squints at me, then pushes a half-filled bowl of cut fruit toward me, letting it scrape along the counter.

"This silly child." He returns to his work at the cutting board. "You make up stories? I can spin one, too: I waited months for my daughter to come back to this house. Every day waiting, waiting. Finally, now that I've seen you, now that you've done the work that only a son or daughter can do for their departed mother, I can return home."

Jiajia is pregnant, I tell him. Does he know this? Does he care?

He makes a performance of shaking his head in disappointment. "Do you believe everything you hear?" he says. "That girl is smarter than you are. She doesn't need our taking care. Look around you. She lives in this big house, even when you or I are not here. Free."

A piece of fruit rolls off the counter and falls to the floor. He bends to collect it and tucks it into his mouth.

. . .

Jiajia remains perfectly stoic as my father's departure date looms. She continues as normal, shuttling from home to work and back. She cooks and cleans. The day before my father's flight, she spends its entirety pulling and kneading a slab of white dough, which she separates into twelve perfectly rotund mantou. These she places in a tall bamboo steamer. I beg her to just sit down for a second, so we can talk, make plans. How will she live? Should she attend college? Does she even want this child? We should make plain what she expects from my father. I can help her. I can be her advocate. I'm not afraid of him.

But she ignores me. And when she can no longer simply ignore me, she evades my questions with that courteous smile of hers. And when that does not deter me, she finally stops what she's doing.

"What is wrong with you?" She slaps her thighs with both hands. I stare at her for a moment, startled, then offer a faltering apology. But her face only deepens in color, glistening from the steam. "Just leave me alone. I'm no one. Look at *yourself*. Take care of *yourself*."

The next day, I drive my father to the airport. We spend most of the ride in silence. He sits with his hands folded in his lap as if he's hiding some prized trinket in the hollow space underneath them.

It's been long enough, I think. Over a decade. We can say anything to each other now; the slate is clean. I could tell him that he'll soon have a grandchild. I could spit in his face. I could steer the car into oncoming traffic. I could tell him I love him, and that he loves me. Simple, like the chorus of a hymnal song.

When we arrive at the concourse, I don't get out of the car. He removes his suitcase from the trunk, and through the passenger side window, we say a stilted goodbye.

29

I go home to Ellis. Where else can I go? There are only two directions: toward love or away from it. He gives me a stern, furrowed brow when I arrive. Upstairs, he won't even look at me as he gets dressed for bed. But in the end Ellis is, as always, quick to forgive. Or, at least, willing to begin the process.

We stay up late, talking, kissing, asking, answering. I tell him about my father, Jiajia, the warehouse. Where does this conversation get us, exactly?

"Nowhere is fine," Ellis says. "We don't have to arrive any place yet."

As usual, it is impossible to resist him, his anodyne. I nuzzle his chest and put my hands on his face. I breathe him in. His skin always smells sweet just after he's showered, like bread. I should have come home sooner.

Yes, he nods. He presses an ice-cold nose to my belly and licks.

. . .

When I wake up the next morning, I'm completely disoriented. I can't exactly remember if I've slept or if I've just lain there with my eyes closed. My eyes are swollen. The skin beneath them is tender and pink. Ellis has already gone to work. On my nightstand, he's placed a mug of coffee. I drink it cold.

Over the next few weeks, my face and hips widen. The skin at my belly stretches and discolors. The spells of dizziness fade, as does the nausea. But my sleep never improves. I wake in the middle of each night, sweaty, choking, desirous. Coursing with frantic energy. The blood in my nose and throat prickles as if threatening to burst forth, but nothing ever happens. No wail, no whimper, no sound. Not even a sneeze.

. . .

I try to visit Jiajia at the house once more. I want to know how she's doing. (In our text messages, she is vague, sometimes entirely unresponsive.) Another part of me wants simply to return to the house. To be within the walls of my mother's home, to feel her missing. There, her absence becomes something tangible. A dearth of her that I can touch and interact with. Ellis offers to accompany me, but I still cannot imagine his presence there as anything but a breach of her wishes.

It's a bright, icy day, and a bracing wind rustles the bare trees and misshapen hedges outside the house. I called Jiajia last week to let her know I was coming, but when I try the front door now, it doesn't budge. My key doesn't fit in the lock.

I call her cell phone; no answer. When I call the house number, an automated voice informs me that its service has been disconnected. I trudge through the uncut grass and hosta leaves that line the side of the house, peering in each window for any sign that she's there. When I knock again, I swear one of the upstairs windows falls dark.

I climb the rotted deck stairs behind the house and try the sliding door by the kitchen, but that's locked, too. Through the glass of the door, I can see a sliver of the kitchen countertops. Pots and pans dry upside down on a rack. A handful of shiitakes soaks in a bowl. One bagel remains in its clear sleeve, which is knotted at the end. On the mat by the door sit Jiajia's shoes—those black, tasseled loafers she wore to the mall.

"Hello." I knock again and again. I try every window I can reach, but none offer any give. I shout, but the house is still, and no one answers me.

. . .

The truth is you cannot return anyplace. Your homeland marches on without you. Your childhood home will fall. Your wife and children do not await your return.

The memory of your mother will not hold. It isn't a memory at all but a fabrication: a projection she lent to the wall for your benefit. She was and remains a stranger, as you both, you understand now, always preferred.

Your husband loves you with or without your assent. Perhaps your love for him takes the same approach. What can you do but give way? To love each other is easy. It's simply to forgive, to accept without qualm. To understand each other is something else entirely.

Your daughter will inherit all the disparate stories you never understood, never even knew. And she will be expected many times over to make herself whole from them. Maybe she'll persevere where you have failed, where you have given up. Isn't that the old, ragged dream?

30

My mother tried to leave us once. We were skating circles at the Arlington Galleria, chasing each other and slamming our bodies into the white wall of the rink. I wore Narisa's old clothes, cuffed at the wrists and ankles. And she wore Mom's in the same style.

Mom watched over us from a bench, holding a white waxen bag filled with gummy candies. We rounded the rink for an umpteenth time, and when our backs were turned, she walked away.

"You didn't even notice I left," she said when we emerged from the rink much later. She wore a terrifying smile. The bag that once held our candies was now crumpled in her hand.

Of course we had seen her. She'd stood and watched us, leaned against the metal railing before turning and rushing away from the bright atrium of the rink. We skated in circles, every time passing that gray, chipped-paint bench where she should have been sitting. It felt like hours had passed, but now I think it couldn't have been that long. Surely either Narisa or I would have said something to someone, to each other.

She watched as we took off our skates. Our feet were sore with blisters. Narisa's white socks were stained red at the Achilles. I limped to the counter for our sneakers.

"I came back, and you didn't even notice. That's how much my children trust me." She shook her head with amazement. "That's how much I've loved them." She insisted on replacing our gummy candies, since, she admitted, she had eaten them all. "They can't imagine I would ever leave. Well, I will not imagine it either."

. . .

The mornings are still dark, but they're getting warmer every day. And when I can't lie still in bed any longer, I slip my sneakers on and walk to Art Park. Today, an early, moonlit breeze reaches around my throat, tickles the back of my neck. I've come to enjoy the particular feeling of cold and moisture in the air at dawn. It's a nice challenge to walk into the wind as if I can head it off at the source.

In the park, I take the long loop that encircles a grove of trees, two playgrounds, a shallow, leaf-strewn pond. A metal gazebo hangs over the water, and near this ugly structure is a row of wooden benches lining the pond's edge.

This is where I first catch sight of that brown coil, like a ratty lock of hair. It lies not three feet from where I stand. A curved, furry "s" in the grass. A disembodied tail. Unmistakably simian. Long, lush, alternating between brown and silver. Is it Sig's?

What am I supposed to do with this? That's my first thought. Why should I be subjected to such an incongruity, such a singular moment that I later will find impossible to believe?

I stare. Water glugs beneath the gazebo's cement platform. Cut reeds whistle faintly along the bank. With two fingers, I lift the stiff, coarse-haired thing from the ground and carry it to the edge of the gazebo. I look for signs of struggle with a predatory creature but find none. No tufts of fur in the grass, no spots of blood along the wood railing.

I let the tail slip like a canoe, like a taut body, onto the surface of the water. Gently. Without a sound. The fur shrinks within seconds, and then the entire thing sinks below. I wonder if I should say a prayer. But what is the point of prayer when the dead and the living are all where they belong?

Birds trill as I limp past their perches. Yellow leaves tumble in my path, and the sky offers its ruddy shades of pink. An ache ripples in my back, which slows me down. Still, I complete the long loop of the park and walk haltingly home.

Author's Note

In some sense, I wrote this book because I was bored of the narrative of immigrants striving and achieving success. I wanted to imagine Asian immigrants (and their second-gen children) who gave up, who relished in all types of quitting—abandonment, cowardice, acquiescence, indifference, self-sabotage. I wanted to interrogate where these behaviors could come from, and where they might lead. I had seen enough of what persistence, ambition, and hard work could (purportedly) do.

A *Quitter's Paradise* interrogates—and sometimes delights in—the cowardice and overintellectualizing of its antihero, Eleanor. (An alternative title for this book, which I seriously considered but which almost everyone thankfully dissuaded me from, was *The Coward*.) This book also explores the hazy and sometimes treacherous dynamics of power and privilege within its family of focus: Rita, Jing, Narisa, Eleanor, Peng, and Jiajia Liu.

The Lius are an American family—some speak English, some speak Mandarin; some hail from Taiwan, others China; some are immigrants, some are not; some have their papers, and some don't. In writing this book, I wanted to explore the experience of difference and othering *within* an immigrant family, as opposed to—or maybe alongside—the particularities of being othered by a nation's dominant culture, say, at work, at school, or among friends.

This book asks if it's possible to understand the self without understanding the family. It wonders if Eleanor might have better understood her own behavior if she had known or contemplated some of the narratives surrounding the rest of her family. Ultimately, only the reader has access to this family's history in its entirety. (This structure of perspective is modeled on James Baldwin's *Go Tell It on the Mountain*, which I am grateful to Alexander Chee for illuminating in a writing class back in 2015.) *A Quitter's Paradise* is interested in the way family histories can distort our senses of self, of agency, of desire, of ambition, and of humanity, even, or perhaps especially, when we don't know what those histories are.

The ending of this book can be read as happy or tragic. I think it depends on whether the reader believes this family, and particularly Eleanor, is worthy of love or condemnation. Both are possible. My hope is that this book is understood as a bit of a collaboration. It invites the reader's judgments and is complete only with the reader's own moral code.

—ELYSHA CHANG

Acknowledgments

Thank you to:

Claudia Ballard, whose wisdom and guidance were vital to this book.

The brilliant Erin Wicks and everyone at Zando who gave this book their energy and expertise.

The Center for Fiction, Kimmel Harding Nelson Center for the Arts, Monson Arts, Swatch Art Peace Hotel, and Willapa Bay AiR for space, time, and support.

Kundiman, especially Sarah Gambito and Joseph O. Legaspi, for showing me true community.

Columbia University School of the Arts, especially Heidi Julavits, Sam Lipsyte, and the tireless Victor LaValle.

Angela Chou and Mitra Heshmati for information and insights that sharpened this book, its people and places.

Sarah Heffner for curbing my worst creative instincts and nurturing my best.

Andrew Eisenman for the years of laughter and sage advice.

Seth Satterlee and Xuan Juliana Wang for reading countless iterations of this book and for seeing its possibilities when I could not.

Anna Chambers, without whose research, intellect, patience, and years of friendship this book would not exist.

Friends and loved ones who encouraged, nourished, inspired, and cared for me as I wrote: Lizzie Harris, Clarisse Baleja Saïdi, Gretchen Gardner, Chiahao Chou, Jeph Fernandez, Josefina Rozenwasser, Sarah Lu, Michelle Caganap, Brian Lee, Sydney Batten, The Perrys, and so many others.

Gu, who has supported me without condition and in so many ways that it is impossible to fully capture here.

My mother and father, who taught me that much of love lies beyond language.

Frank, the great protector of my time and energies. With you, all things come to life.

About the Author

ELYSHA CHANG has received fellowships from the Center for Fiction and Kundiman. A graduate of Columbia University's School of the Arts, her writing has been published in *Fence*, *GQ*, the *Rumpus*, and others. She has taught Asian American literature and creative writing at Villanova University and the University of Pennsylvania. She lives in Brooklyn with her family.